USA TODA

Dale Mayer

TERK'S GUARDIANS

ROYAL 09

ROYAL: TERK'S GUARDIANS, BOOK 9
Beverly Dale Mayer
Valley Publishing Ltd.

ISBN-13: 978-1-778864-80-3
Print Edition

Books in This Series:

Radar, Book 1

Legend, Book 2

Bojan, Book 3

Langdon, Book 4

Walker, Book 5

Reid, Book 6

Sanders, Book 7

Nate, Book 8

Royal, Book 9

Alex, Book 10

About This Book

A prisoner of the Kremlin and of a failed exchange several years ago, Royal is losing hope of ever being free again—particularly when the firing squad date is already set for his execution. He has exhausted all avenues of escape. Now it seems to be the end of the line …

Janna has been through way-too-much pain and anguish recently, and yet somehow she can't walk away from helping Royal, even though he'd walked away from her a long time ago. Maybe because she has nothing left to care about, this would be her last gift to give—if someone can just get to Royal in time.

Time is against them. Conditions are against them. Enemies are against them. Can they fight the odds, and, in the process, save themselves?

PROLOGUE

IN THE KITCHEN, seated among some other members of his team at the huge dining table, Terkel shuffled through the paperwork before him and still smiled when Natalia handed him a large accounting binder. He shoved it back at her. "Just give me the CliffsNotes version."

She laughed. "The CliffsNotes are in this binder," she stated. "That satellite is damn important to us."

"It is and it isn't," he replied. "The world's a mess, and we can use two satellites owned by our generous friends, but if one of them goes down—"

"I understand," she said, "so we need to keep working toward putting away funding for our own. So more jobs would be good."

He rolled his eyes at that. "We also need to sustain our ability to crew these ops, without sending everybody out on these other jobs."

"Which we seem to be doing so far, especially with the help of Levi's and Bullard's teams," she noted, with a chuckle. "Other jobs are coming in, right?"

Terk nodded. "Actually, a local job is next, but I'm not too sure how to handle it yet."

"Why is that?"

"It involves a woman with abilities, someone I've talked to in the past. However, she's never been very up-front and open about joining our group. Yet she contacted me a few days ago and wants our help."

"What kind of help, and does she have money to pay us?" He laughed.

"She does have money. She was an influencer for a long time, made millions of dollars, then disappeared from public view. When I checked in on her, she told me that she was fine, yet she was putting off this *stay away* energy about her."

"What about now?" Clary asked, as she got up from the huge dining table to get more coffee and then moved closer to the discussion at hand. "It's always fascinating when a woman's involved."

"Lately it seems as if a woman is always involved," Terk stated, with a sigh. "It's that whole *Love Boat* thing going on again."

"I think you can blame Levi for that," Clary noted, with a laugh.

"Maybe." Terk grinned at the thought. "Anyway, her name is Janna, and her problem, at least according to her, is that somebody keeps contacting her that they need help, but she doesn't know where they are. Now it's gotten to the point where she can't function."

"Who is contacting Janna?"

"Somebody she used to know a long time ago. They were lovers for a while, and then he disappeared and went off into some military training. Something happened after that," he explained. "I'm waiting for the file to come in. I told her I wouldn't even look at it until I had more information, and she said she had no choice but to help as much as she could, since she knows him. Plus he's locked on to her energy, and she hasn't been able to shake loose of him."

"She wants to shake loose?"

"She wants to, but I'm not exactly sure why. She's coming in today to talk to me."

"So, she is local?"

"She is."

At that, Sophia walked into the kitchen with a woman at her side. The visitor was dressed in jeans and a T-shirt, with a huge cardigan pulled up around her neck. She had masses of bright red hair, and she looked at Terkel expectantly.

Terkel stood up and studied her face. "Janna?"

She nodded slowly. "How can you even recognize me?" she asked bitterly. "Look at my face."

"I see your face," he stated, "and, yes, I've seen your previous photos as well. Why don't you tell me what happened."

She shrugged. "A fan found out where I lived and threw acid in my face," she shared. "I went underground and away from the world for a long time, right up until I started getting these calls."

Terk nodded. "Did you bring your information?"

She held out a folder and nodded. "This is all I have on him, all that I have recorded of his memories, and anything else I could get my hands on."

He nodded and asked, "And you're prepared for whatever reception you get?"

"I don't have a choice," she admitted. "I already know what it's like for people to see my face and stare. If I could do anything more about it, I would, but I can't do a whole lot else. This is what I'm left with. Meanwhile, I can't leave him alone, so I have no choice but to come out of my safe and secluded existence and deal with it."

"Why is that?"

She frowned and looked down at her hands.

Terkel added, "We need to know, Janna."

"He was the father of my one and only child," she replied, "who died of heart issues seven years ago. He didn't know there was a child, and he didn't know about our son's death either. I guess I feel as if I owe him. He gave me a wonderful gift, even if it was a gift I couldn't keep," she added, tears in her eyes.

"Go on."

"And now that he needs help, I can't just walk away."

"I get it," Terk replied, then looked over at the others gathered at the table. "Are you guys ready to take a look at this case?" They nodded, and, almost as if he'd made an announcement over a loudspeaker, more people started to filter into the massive dining room.

Janna stared in shock as more and more people gathered. "Terkel?"

"Yeah." He nodded, smiling with pride. "The team … grew."

"I guess that's a good thing?" she said doubtfully.

"It's a *great* thing," he declared, pulling out a chair for her. "Take a seat, and welcome to the family."

CHAPTER 1

JANNA MONROE STARED across at Rick, her expression calm, almost blank, but that was the default expression she used as she stared out at the world. They were still in the castle, still at Terk's huge dining table in the kitchen. She'd even shared a meal with them, as they'd tried to regroup forces. Rick would be her partner in this rescue mission, but he obviously wasn't happy about it. She continued to study him.

"It really would be better if you just stayed here," he stated, glaring at her for the umpteenth time.

"That may very well be true," she conceded, "but you won't find Royal without me." He groaned, and she shrugged, as if she hadn't a care in the world. "Unless you have a finder on board here."

Immediately everybody turned to Langdon.

So, he must be their finder, Janna thought to herself. *Interesting.* She read Langdon's energy and shrugged. "He is indeed a finder, but not the same as I am."

"And that means what?" Rick asked.

"It means that I'm locked on to Royal's energy. While I may not know his actual location, I know which direction we should be heading," she shared, looking from one to another. "Your guy Langdon might have other skills that we could use to make this work easier, but the chances of finding Royal without me are not very good."

"Do you know what happened to him?" Clary asked, patting her tummy gently.

Janna shifted her gaze away from Clary's rotund belly, just one of so many here that made Janna's heart clamp with grief and despair. She shook her head. "No, all I'm getting from him is that he was doing a job for some government agency," she explained, trying desperately to hold back her emotions. Still, such bitterness came through her tone—a bitterness she hadn't been prepared to let surface—as the others faced her. She clamped down her jaw and glared at Terk.

He took a moment and looked around at the rest of them. "One of the reasons Janna wouldn't come work as part of the team some years back was because she has had some issues with government agencies."

The note of humor in his tone surprised her. Puzzled, Janna stared at him oddly. "And yet you don't appear to be … Surely this property wasn't provided for by the US government?"

He shook his head. "Right, you are correct," he declared, his tone calm, reflective even, as he studied her. "We definitely found some downsides to being tethered to government affiliations."

She snorted at that statement. "I had a taste of it, remember? No backup. No support. Only take, take, take," she muttered. "That was not what I would do and definitely not something I signed up for. I did one job for them and walked."

"Not too happily either, as I recall."

"No, I basically ran before I didn't have anything left to even walk away with," she stated, staring at him, "as you very well know."

"I do know," Terk confirmed, with a small smile, "and that was a bad deal." He looked around at the others and clarified, "Janna was asked to work in Germany on a special project, but it ended up being quite an abusive job situation, as the researcher didn't believe in the work that we were doing, that Janna was doing," Terk corrected and then sighed. "She ended up a prisoner, then escaped to get out of Dodge, so to speak."

"Yeah, ya think?" Janna quipped, with a shudder. "A lot of those government workers cannot be trusted."

"A lot of them aren't trustworthy," Terk agreed. "We went through that exact same hell ourselves." And then he told her what had happened to them with the CIA and the others. All of it.

She stared, dumbfounded, her gaze going from one team member to the next, getting hard nods and cold looks in return. "Good God, yet you're doing jobs for them now?"

"On our terms and within our business model," Terk noted, with a smirk, "because, as you know, governments have lots of money. And money is money, no matter who is paying the bill."

She blinked at him and then giggled. "Oh, now that's a really good thing. I'm glad to hear that it works for you because, wow, if I thought that you were still working for those guys ..."

"We're not exactly what you would call *working* for them," he clarified, with a wry smile. "We are, in a sense, on a contract basis, but we set the terms. We have our freedom, and we are free to refuse them, if that is our choice."

"Good," Janna declared, "because I'm pretty sure a government agency has Royal."

At that, some of them stiffened.

"What are you talking about?" Rick asked.

She sighed. "I think he's in Russia, … but I'm not sure. He went over there as part of a group to do a job, and then … I don't know what happened."

"How do you even know that much?"

She flushed. "I've kept track of him … on the ethers," she admitted. "I know it's stupid, and I will not tolerate any criticism from you on this matter. However, after losing my child, it seemed to be the only way I could heal, by keeping a connection open to Samuel's father."

The women nodded at Janna, and she knew Terk was studying her energy with that same in-depth ability that he always had, but still, she glared at him. "Yes, that probably makes me psychotic when I refused to have any other connection with Royal, and it also probably makes me look unstable even, but I really don't give a shit."

Terk's lips twitched. "I always liked that about you. A lot of people thought you were just bitchy and bitter. As far as I am concerned, you were always a straight shooter."

"Always have been," she stated. "That hasn't changed. Losing my son was the most incredibly devastating event of my life," she shared, "and I became incredibly protective of all forms of life ever since, though I'd always been that way to some degree. I had six months with my baby, and that was it." She looked away from all of them. "All the while I was trying to figure out whether I should tell Royal about Samuel or not."

"What makes you think he didn't already know?" Rick asked, his tone cool, obviously not appreciating the fact that the child's father had been kept out of the loop.

"Royal took off," Janna snapped, "before I even learned I

was pregnant, and I never heard from him again."

"What kind of time line can you give us on all this?" Terk asked.

"My government work was around ten years ago. The incident with the acid was shortly thereafter. Then I had … maybe a million surgeries over the next couple years to fix my face. Royal came into my life around eight years ago, and I got pregnant," she shared, with a wave of her hand. She took a deep breath.

"I was lonely, felt hated by the world, and very unattractive, thinking I would never have a relationship ever again in my life. Yet I gave in at a weak moment, and Royal and I had a wild and crazy weekend, which did a lot to reopen some of the pathways I had shut off. When our weekend was over, … he was supposed to call me. Of course he didn't. So, I went through all kinds of drama. *Screw him. He didn't care anyway.* I'm sure you can imagine how that went," she said, looking at the women, who all nodded.

"What happened then?" Terk asked.

"When I realized I was pregnant, I did try to reach out to him and got no response," she stated bitterly. "I got nothing on the energy pathways that we had opened and had shared up until then. Nothing. I didn't know what to think, and I went through the pregnancy alone—the highs, the lows, still trying to contact Royal. After Samuel was born, I gave up trying to contact Royal, as my hands were full.

"Samuel was born with a heart condition, and he had lots of issues. The doctors were still running tests, trying to figure out exactly what the problem was, when he just … didn't make it. One night he went to sleep as always and … never woke up again." At this point, she couldn't hold back the tears. She sniffled several times. "I'm sorry. I keep thinking that I'll talk about him and not cry the next time. Yet … I just can't."

And then two of the most beautiful women she'd ever seen in the world, clearly twins, moved to sit down on either side of her. They each gently picked up one of her hands and placed Janna's hands on their protruding tummies.

The tears welled up again, and Janna sniffled.

"I'm Clary and this is my sister, Cara. Just because you suffered a loss," Clary whispered, "doesn't mean you won't find joy again. It doesn't mean you won't have another child. Yet each one will be different, of course, because each child will be a different soul. However, your son Samuel has moved on, and he is at peace. You should never blame yourself for his death."

Janna stared at Clary and whispered, "I know. It's the only thing that helped me survive this. I saw him leave. I was in the room with him and was just nodding off myself. I woke up suddenly and saw this shimmering energy atop my son's body. I cried out, begging him not to leave, begging him to take me along, and he gave me the sweetest smile, almost as if … a kiss in the wind, and then he was gone. I'll be the first to admit that I haven't been the same since."

"I can only imagine," Cara replied, teary herself.

"In the meantime, I've had no contact from Royal, at least not until several weeks ago," she explained, "and I've done everything I could to reply, to reach him, but I can't. Also I've tried everything I could to block him out, and I can't do that either." Janna waved her hands in frustration. "At that point I decided, if I desire any sanity to return to my world, I would have to do something to help him."

"Yet otherwise you're against helping him?" Rick asked in that same hard tone.

"It's not that I'm against it," Janna clarified, "but I understand what I'm supposed to do. I'm confused, yet I want to help Royal, even if for a sense of closure. So that is why I came to Terk, because it's very much more in your wheelhouse."

"It's exactly our wheelhouse," Rick confirmed, "which is also why I don't want you coming."

"That's nice," she snapped, stiffening her back and raising her chin in a move everybody recognized. "Yet I am coming along with you, so get used to it."

"You seem sensible. So I hope you don't have a death wish—or do you?" Rick asked in that same hard tone.

"No, I do not have a death wish. Do I have a burning desire to live? No, not particularly. I haven't found the world all that hospitable," she declared fiercely. "However, I don't blame Royal, even though I don't know what happened to us. Yet I'm not trying to fit into some righteous victim narrative either. Besides, it's way past time to do anything about my life anyway. Samuel is long gone, and I certainly won't be looking for love or to get pregnant again," Janna muttered.

"I can only handle so much pain, and frankly I'm well past my limit for that. If you don't want to help me, I get it, fine. However, not helping me is one thing, but not helping Royal is another." Frazzled, she turned to Terk, with a head tilt to Rick, as if asking who the hell this guy was. With the tiniest headshake, she got herself back to the matter at hand. "But back to Royal. You should remember him, Terk. You looked at bringing him on board many years ago."

He frowned at her. "Really? I don't remember him."

"You will remember Royal if you ever see his energy again," she noted, with half a smile. "I'm not sure what's happened to him and why he's in this situation, but I can tell you that he's reaching out."

Just then Terk's phone rang. He frowned as he stared down at an all-too-familiar number, one they all knew to be the CIA. He held it up for the rest of his team to see, at least those who were closest, and their frowns were instant.

"You can deep-six that number." One of the men, she thought his name was Damon, declared with a hard tone. "We don't need to be taking calls from those bastards. I vote you block it."

"We all know very well that I can't do that," Terk replied mildly, seemingly unbothered. He got up and walked a short distance away from the group to take the call.

Janna could only stare and watch as the others, filled with mixed emotions, stared daggers at Terk's back. "The US government, I presume," Janna muttered. "I don't know anybody else who can cause that kind of universal reaction."

Clary turned to Janna and chuckled. "You're quite correct. That's definitely who it is." She smiled at the woman. "You do know that healing starts from within, right?"

Rolling her eyes, Janna nodded. "I've been working on it, but sometimes it just seems as if we can't heal so many things. We can't see that things will ever improve. And some days, with all that failure staring me in the face, quite literally, I just give up. Why bother? I didn't want to live without my son, but guess what? I'm still here," she stated bitterly. "It's not as if anybody's listening."

"Of course you feel that way. We all would. As you have no doubt noticed, we're all very much in the family way around here, hoping these precious lives will go smoothly. But there are no guarantees in life. No matter what, we live with whatever life has in store for us. We also know that the healing work we do …" She hesitated, then glanced at her sister. "Both my sister and I frequently work with people very much on the verge of death, and … sometimes we must let them go."

Janna stared from Clary to Cara and back again. Janna felt as if she had been splashed with ice water but was too stunned to say anything.

Clary continued. "Sometimes it's what they need, and sometimes it's what they want. In your case, I don't know what happened with Samuel. All I can tell you is that, when death does come, we do believe it's for the right reason."

Janna dropped her head and nodded. "I've been to hell and back trying to convince myself of that, but somehow it still doesn't make it any easier."

"I understand," Clary replied. "Still, we could do a lot to help you heal."

"Heal me? In what way?" Janna asked, frowning at her. "I haven't worked with energy healers before. I didn't know any who were truly gifted. Most of them … Well, does the word *charlatan* come to mind?" she asked, with a bitter laugh. "No offense."

Clary nodded. "Definitely a lot of those are out there, but I can assure you that we are not of that bent and would certainly be willing to do whatever we could to help you heal from that devastating hurt."

"But in what way could you help me heal?" Janna asked, looking at the twins oddly.

They smiled. "One of the things that's the hardest to understand is that healing comes from within. We know how much pain you're in and how little healing can happen because of that agony." Clary added, "So, if you would give us a few days, we can set your perspective straight."

"When?" Janna asked. "I'll go help them find Royal, so afterward maybe? Yet I always pay a price when rehashing those memories of loss. However, when I return with Royal, I'll probably be more willing to pay it."

The two women exchanged a glance, then faced Janna. "You're totally okay if you don't come back from this mission, aren't you?"

Janna shrugged. "Not very much in my world is worth staying connected to," she admitted. "Now, before you get all hyped up, the way Rick over there did, let me be clear. I don't have a death wish, and I'm not trying to get myself killed on this job," she repeated, with a smile. "I'm doing this to give Royal a chance at a better life than mine. And, yes, I'm conflicted. I don't really want to open that door and all the hurt that will come rushing in again. And I, … I guess that might come across as being suicidal, but I'm not."

Janna gave another wave of her hand. "You need to understand that I'm really not suicidal. I promise. I guess I'm just fatalistic, and my perspective isn't all that great. I can't see much on this side of life that's realistically worth living for. Look at you. You're all in relationships. You're all at the start of a brand-new life, which, for you, is incredibly exciting and fascinating," she shared, looking around at all of them.

"Now look at me. Look at my face. The last relationship I had was with Royal, who then promptly left me. In fairness, we didn't have any permanent plans, but, yes, he was supposed to contact me, and he didn't. So, what do you think I assumed was the reason?"

"Yet you don't know what his reason was. You don't even know whether or not the reason was within his control," Clary added, and then studied Janna's face intently.

"You know, living tissue is still there."

"Sure, and the doctor told me that I can go back for several more rounds of surgery when I'm up for it," she replied, with a snicker. "As if it's that simple or that easy." She shook her head. "I haven't done any surgeries since Samuel passed, and, at this point, I, … I really don't care to do any more."

She got up and paced the small room. "Look. I know that Terk's on the phone, and I know that you guys need him to be a part of this discussion, but I also need to be a part of this Royal mission too," she stated. "I really don't think you'll survive rescuing Royal without me."

At that, Terk walked back over to the table, pocketing his phone. "Why is that?" he asked, eyeing her intently.

"I don't know," she admitted, "except for the connection between us."

Terk sighed. "You were correct about that call. … That was the US government, the CIA. They are the same old agency but with new people in charge," he shared, with an eye roll at the rest of his team. "They have also expressed an interest in getting Royal out. Apparently he's being held—compliments of the Kremlin—in a prison. The CIA was trying to do a prisoner exchange, which has been refused. The Kremlin states Royal is treasonous, and they want to execute him."

Janna gasped at that.

Terk nodded. "The trouble with that comment is that it causes lots of drama, but it doesn't really do us any good. So, the CIA has asked us to help free Royal—illegally of course. So, we will take on this op, and it is totally off the books." He turned and looked at the others. "Thoughts?"

"Janna was willing to pay, so we don't need the CIA's money in the first place," Rick pointed out. "I'm willing to go. I speak some Russian, though I'm not that great at it. Still, that's not an issue right now. I would just as soon not come across any Russians, if we have a choice in the matter."

Terk nodded at that. "We definitely don't want to encounter any of them if we can help it," he murmured. "Yet dealing with the locals is our normal approach."

"We never get any answers from the Russian people," Rick noted. "You know that. We all do. And so finding those answers could be a bit harder, especially if Royal's in rough shape."

"He is definitely in rough shape," Janna stated. "That's another reason why I need to go. We need to get to him fast."

At that tidbit, everybody eyed her questioningly.

She sighed. "When we were together, I realized I could … help him heal. I don't know why him or even how I did it. I don't understand how any of that works, but, after we were separated, I used that energy to try and connect with his energy. The fact that he was ignoring me made me angry, but it didn't change the fact that we have a connection."

"And you think you can help heal him via that connection? If so, can you heal him from here?" Clary asked urgently. "Can you give Royal energy? Can you do anything at all from a distance right now?"

"I don't know," Janna admitted. "I've never tried to do this."

"You need to try it then. It'll take a little bit of time for our team to get the logistics in place and to sort out things with the CIA," Clary explained, turning to Terk. "I presume an urgency is attached to this."

"Yes, there is. Royal's slated for a firing squad next week," he told them.

Everybody turned to look at Janna. She was at a loss for words and just shook her head.

Terk turned to Janna and yet kept a watchful eye on Rick, "I get that you want to go, Janna …"

At that, Rick started protesting.

Terk held up a hand. "I'll send a couple of you with Janna to ensure this goes as planned. However, we don't even have a plan yet. So, with more of you on board, maybe we can reach Royal faster." He turned to the others. "Volunteers?"

Calum nodded. "I'll go. Those Russian jails are the worst."

"And, if Royal's an American and a political prisoner, you can guarantee the Russians haven't been easy on him," Rick shared, as everybody turned to Janna.

She nodded. "He is in rough shape, but he is there. I just don't know what that means."

Clary noted, "You need to tell us exactly what you're feeling as to Royal's situation and exactly what you think is going on with his system. If we can get those details, we may be able to give Royal some support from here."

Cara nodded in affirmation.

When Janna frowned at the twins, clearly puzzled, Clary nodded. "We heal. That's what we do. It's … who we are and how we operate, but we do it in a big way, and we can do it from here."

Janna still stared at them.

"Yes, from here, and that keeps us safe. It keeps our children safe," Clary clarified, with a laugh.

"And we don't have much choice," Cara added, with a light laugh. "As round as we are, we don't necessarily want to be on the front lines anyway. However, we have gone out and done several jobs onsite, depending on who was involved and the circumstances. Yet, for the duration of our pregnancies, that's not really in the plans."

"No, I wouldn't think so," Janna agreed, staring at the women. "Still, I'm surprised that you're even considering being involved at all. You don't even know who Royal is."

"It doesn't matter," Clary declared. "Not all of the world is inhospitable and angry, and you've come from many horrific scenarios in your past that hurt you. And trying to heal when you've got as many issues as you're dealing with," she explained in a calm tone, "can be very difficult, but it's not impossible, and we can help you. We would prefer that you stay here, but you're arguing against that pretty clearly. So I presume you have a reason for that."

"Yes, and I'm not arguing against it for my sake. I'm arguing because I *need* to go. I have to. I see no option."

And, with that, Terk nodded. "So, that ends the argument." He looked around at the others. "We need to get plans in motion. You'll be outta here soon." He checked his watch and then asked Sophia, "We need flights. Can you check that out?"

Sophia nodded. "On it, now that I know how many are going."

"Immediately, and private if we can," Terk added. "We'll need our people to land as near to Russia as possible, preferably without anybody knowing."

Sophia laughed. "Now this sounds like fun," she quipped, flexing her fingers. "I'll set up aliases and get the IDs ready." And, with that, she quickly disappeared.

Terk faced Janna. "You need to sleep." When she shook her head, he frowned at her. "The time to argue has passed, and you've just hit that wall." She glared at him, and he smiled. "You're worried, and I get that, and I'm happy that you came to us for help. The fact is, the CIA will pick up the tab, so that makes it even easier, but the bottom line is that you're still in rough shape, and we'll need you up to par for this op, as much as you can be, before you leave." He walked to her side and then added with finality, "So, go get some rest while you can. Clary and Cara can show you to a spare bedroom."

And, with that, he turned and looked at the others. "If any of you guys can do anything to help, you know the drill."

Then he turned and walked out of the room, with Calum and Rick following at his heels.

ROYAL HENDERSON SANK back against the single cot, furnished with a single thin *blanket*. It was more a sheet than a blanket, but the guards called it a blanket more to mock their prisoners than anything. Royal glanced over at his cellmate, a dangerously thin man, probably five years younger than Royal was, and in worse shape, so Royal kept funneling more energy his way to try and keep the poor guy alive.

"I won't last much longer," Bruce muttered.

"Yes, you will," Royal declared, determined to keep his friend bolstered. "If not, we'll both go out together." Royal snorted. "And I'm scheduled to go out next week, right?"

"They've been telling us about our executions being planned for months now, but, so far, it hasn't happened. It's propaganda, trying to work their psychological games on us."

"That may be, but this time it feels different somehow."

"No, they just like to torment us," Bruce argued, shifting on the single cot. "One good thing about dying though. At least I won't be so damn cold," he muttered.

"The cold is jarring, isn't it? We can never find a comfortable position to be warm. If we ever did, we would probably sleep. Of course sleep deprivation is part of their torture as well."

"Sleeping wouldn't be a bad thing either. It's not as if we've had any sleep in a very long time."

"Not beyond dozing with one eye open, that's for sure," Royal clarified, "but even that isn't easy in here."

Royal stared around at the small room, roughly eight by six, with two identical cots chained up against opposite walls. Just the two of them were here, so they hardly had any space to move. Royal was pretty sure that he and Bruce were being monitored, which is why he spoke mostly telepathically with the seemingly comatose young man on the cot beside him. Royal knew that the time was coming when the young man wouldn't make it, and yet Royal was doing everything he could to keep Bruce alive, but it was damn hard.

It broke his heart every time he saw Bruce fade away a little bit more. Royal kept funneling more and more energy toward him, not for the first time wishing that he had more skills, more education, more of any knowledge whatsoever about energy work, so that it would help Bruce more.

Royal also knew that, as soon as Bruce died, Royal's own energy would surge in a big way. Without the tether keeping Bruce alive, maybe Royal could get himself out of here. However, sacrificing somebody else's life in order to save himself was crossing a line. Even if Royal were able to get himself out of here, no way he could ever get back in to help Bruce. Therefore, Royal was stuck where he was, doing the best he could to keep the young man alive for as long as possible, meanwhile hoping some help appeared before one or both of them died in here. This place was just a dark hole. Standing by and letting someone die was something Royal simply could not do.

When someone was taken prisoner by the Russians, execution usually happened pretty quickly. Yet Royal suspected some negotiations were happening, some jockeying back and forth. It could involve potential trades for other people. He didn't know for sure, but it seemed as if he'd been here for a year. More likely it was probably about ten months. He'd lost track of time, and things were sometimes a little hard for him to figure out, particularly when he was funneling all this energy to Bruce.

When the wooden door to the cell slammed open, he didn't move. It slammed open on a regular basis as buckets were brought in and out. Swill was brought in and given to them, plus water, the ever-present water, which wasn't usually drinkable, but Royal and Bruce had no choice, so whatever.

Their jailer greeted them with raucous laughter. "This one will not even make it to the firing squad next week," he declared, still laughing. "They'll save some bullets with him."

Royal almost winced at that, hearing the reference to next week. It wasn't the first time he'd heard about that, but this time he did register it. Maybe it was finally time. As soon as the door slammed shut again, he looked over at Bruce.

His cellmate nodded, then whispered in his mind, *See? I won't make it.*

You'll make it, Royal argued, wishing he could believe it himself. Bruce didn't deserve this. None of them did. But the Russians were the Russians, and they had their own code, their own rules and laws. Nobody got a chance to even argue their case because they were just taken out back and shot.

At least that's all Royal had seen from this nightmare. He had come over, supposedly to do a job with the CIA, working with an intelligence department. Instead he had been jailed almost immediately after the job ended and labeled a traitor. He shifted, his own body in agony due to the nonexistent protection offered by the bare cot with a single sheet, and getting far too skinny himself, fragile even. He hated to even consider how fragile he had become. He shifted once more, trying to get comfortable, his mind working around next week's scheduled execution. He wondered if he was the reason that date had been pushed back several times.

He'd hoped so because it gave him a flicker of optimism, but he figured other people were playing games and trying to get something out of keeping him alive. Maybe they'd given up on negotiating now. Royal didn't know. He looked over at Bruce and frowned. It was hard to see if he was breathing, so Royal got up and checked for a pulse. It was there but very faint. "Hang on, Bruce," Royal whispered. "Come on. Hang on, buddy. You can make it, man."

Realistically he knew Bruce had a pretty slim chance of surviving this ordeal, and that thought just made Royal angry. Angry and hurt that some young man—who had done absolutely nothing wrong—could be in this position and at the mercy of the bitter and angry men at the Kremlin, where nobody cared. As long as Bruce didn't cause them trouble, they were okay to let him suffer here, until he faded away into nothing.

Frustrated, Royal got up yet again and walked over to

the food bucket on the floor. It contained some watery gruel, the only thing that they ever got. It clearly didn't come with vitamins or nutrients. It was usually hard to get down, and he only ate it because he needed something to keep himself alive, even though it was getting increasingly more difficult for his stomach to accept.

He closed his eyes and just ate, not even allowing himself to think about what he was eating. When he heard an odd sound, he walked over to Bruce, placing a hand on his shoulder, telling him, "It's okay, buddy. It's okay."

The other man shifted, which was one of the biggest signs of life he'd seen out of Bruce in a long time. Royal bent down beside him. "Hey, Bruce, you awake?"

Bruce's eyes slowly opened, and he looked at him briefly. Then he shut them quickly and whispered, "I wish I wasn't."

"Can you eat?"

He shook his head. "No, it won't stay down. I just want to go back to sleep."

"I thought for sure you were in a coma, so the fact that you're even talking to me is something."

"We've been talking," he muttered. "I know we have been."

Royal didn't say anything to that because they had been, just not talking consciously. They'd been talking in a way that he wasn't sure Bruce could handle, even if he knew.

"That's right. I'm just trying to keep you in good spirits. Better try some water at least." With that, he brought some and tried to help him get down a swallow or two. "Sure you don't want to try and get some of this other down?"

Bruce opened his eyes and asked, "Why? They'll kill us one way or the other. It's just so painful while they make up their minds. I wish they would decide pretty damn soon. I'm sick of this." Bruce shivered and fell silent.

Royal walked back to his own bunk and grabbed his sheet and wrapped it around his friend's shoulders.

The other man sighed and sank back under again.

It was good that Bruce had been awake for a bit. It was truly sad that Bruce was right in the sense that this was just a painfully endless dawdling torture, to the point that Bruce would be grateful to have it all over with. And that just pissed off Royal all over again. For weeks, he had been sending out messages to anybody out there, hoping maybe somebody would hear him.

And yet he wasn't getting any response at all, … from anybody. He looked down at Bruce and sent more energy his way, trying to keep him bolstered and in good spirits. Exhausted and too gloomy to continue, Royal sank back down onto his bed, now without a cover, knowing, even if he fell asleep, he might end up with pneumonia. He quickly made a decision and walked over to Bruce, lying down behind him, giving him the benefit of his body heat, even as they shared the two sheets. Then Royal closed his eyes and fell asleep again.

CHAPTER 2

JANNA WALKED OFF the plane. As her foot landed on the tarmac, she looked around and announced, "He's not alone."

Calum looked at her, at least acknowledging she had spoken.

Up until now, he and Rick hadn't had a whole lot to do with her. Rick didn't want her here, and he didn't trust her, at least not enough, and she knew that. Still, she had no choice but to be here for this op.

"He's not alone," she repeated. "I don't know what other people are with him, as in another prisoner or what the deal is. However, I can tell you that another energy is around him."

"The gals are trying to pinpoint Royal's location," Calum shared. "They were trying to piggyback onto your connection to Royal, so maybe they can find him that way."

"I hope so," Janna muttered, chewing on her bottom lip. "Something is off about that other person. Maybe it is another prisoner, one who's in tough shape, even worse than Royal."

"And Royal?" Calum asked.

"He's alive," she replied. "I'm not too sure beyond that."

Calum nodded. "We'll see what we can find out."

She frowned at Calum and shook her head. "I don't get

it. How the hell will you arrange to get him out of a Russian prison?" she asked bitterly, knowing all the while it was wrong to be so cranky with these men who were willingly putting themselves at risk to help her.

Calum laughed. "The one advantage is they are mostly all corrupt to some degree. Therefore, if you can find somebody who's crooked as all hell, you can pretty well purchase anything you want in Russia, and that includes freedom."

"So, if that's the case, then why didn't the US government already do just that?" she asked in shock. "If they could have bought Royal's freedom, why haven't they?"

"Because the price in this case is bound to be pretty high, probably too high. The alternative is that the Russians haven't recognized that Royal's even a prisoner. Another possibility is perhaps the Russians told our government that Royal died, and his body was burned up in an accident or something. They use any number of excuses continuously to drag out negotiations, without any care in the world as to whether it's the truth or not."

"Remember that part about my hating governments?" Janna muttered.

"Yeah, I know about that," Calum replied, "and I get it. I also get that you've got a good reason for it. So does our team. However, I'm also here to tell you that a whole lot more than just governments and agencies operate in the shadows."

"Maybe," she conceded, "but I can't say I've seen a whole lot of good come from any of that either."

"Maybe not, but you can't stay bitter forever. You are killing yourself from the inside."

At that, she buttoned her lips. It's not that she was bitter—well, maybe she was—but it wasn't the dominant feeling. She just wanted nothing to do with anybody. So maybe *apathy* was what she felt, or *indifference*. After being burned and disfigured so terribly, she had turned inward, eventually building herself back up from scratch. It was hard to trust after something so horrific. Then, when the authorities had let her attacker spend the rest of their life in a nice and comfortable little mental hospital, while Janna spent her life in uncomfortable surgical hospitals, yet still looking the way she did, it didn't make her feel any better.

The fact that her attacker was also now deceased just added fuel to the fire somewhat, and that made Janna feel even worse because she still wanted to exact her revenge. She was supposed to be a good person, and yet it was darn hard sometimes to find that goodness when so much bitterness remained inside her still. She felt such bitterness over the acid attack, but then Samuel's birth had changed things. She cherished him. When Sam was born, she was so thrilled and happy, even appreciating her weekend with Royal to beget such a gift. However, when Sam passed away, it just amplified her pain and the ugliness from the acid attack tenfold.

She had been seeing somebody to help her deal with her facial scars and the aftermath of Sam's passing, but they had parted ways over not agreeing with a treatment strategy. The woman wanted Janna on medication in order to find her happy place, but Janna had always been totally against medicating herself out of life. That never worked.

At least in her experience it hadn't, and she wasn't prepared to sit here and to end up half a person because of the drugs she was on. If she couldn't trust herself without the drugs, she didn't want to try to trust herself with them. It made no sense to her that the professional would be so quick to advocate prescription treatment. When she had tried to protest that she wanted to do this with a natural method and actually deal with her problems, the doctor had looked at her with sympathy and then had told her there was no dealing with it, that she was well beyond that point.

That was something else Janna didn't like, that whole defeatist mind-set. But again, nobody was listening to Janna. She walked out of that session and never went back. Thankfully nobody had the power to force her to go back either. When the office called to set up the next appointment, Janna just told them that she had chosen a different therapist. It was her choice after all, and, from then on, that had been the end of it … thankfully.

Even now she could work herself into quite a temper over her treatment by that therapist, yet it wouldn't do any good. It never did any good. That was part of the problem that Janna struggled with—the fact that you could do everything right in life, and still … shit happened.

Shit that you didn't do anything to deserve, but it didn't matter one bit. It all still happened, and it was still there, and you were left to deal with it, whether you liked it or not. Caught up in her own thoughts and hating the fact that she was once again having that conversation in her mind, she was startled when a tap came on her shoulder. She frowned at Calum, motioning at a car.

She quickly slipped into the back seat of the vehicle. They'd flown into Poland, rented a car, and now would drive from here. She also knew that the car wouldn't get them very far. But they couldn't afford to let anybody in Russia know that they were arriving—or that anybody at all was arriving from the US. More shocking was the fact that she was with two guys with former ties to the CIA. That was typically a big no-no in her world, but past ties were one thing. The fact that the CIA had hired Terkel's team and were funding this operation was even more shocking to her, and it boggled her mind that she was involved. Now they would find a way across the border and pick up wheels on the other side.

As they drove forward, she looked around and noted, "We're going in the wrong direction."

Calum nodded. "True, but ultimately we still get across the border. So let's focus on that, until you can give us a better direction."

She pondered that and nodded. "That makes sense. I guess we get across the border first and go from there."

"Sounds like a plan to me," he replied cheerfully, and then he studied her for a moment. "The dark hair looks good on you."

She laughed. "The shorter haircut is what I liked the most. With the bangs and large sunglasses, I can hide some of the disfiguration. It's too bad we still aren't wearing masks everywhere. That would have gone a long way to hiding my face too."

"You worry about how your face looks too much," Calum said. "However, the reality is, it does make you identifiable, and that's really the only concern we have amid this op. As far as looks go, it's not all that bad. *Really.*"

She frowned at him in surprise.

He shrugged. "*Seriously.* You've probably seen it as this ravaging scar for so long that you haven't noticed that it has healed a lot, has calmed down quite a bit, and is quite likely much improved from what it was initially."

"It doesn't feel improved," she argued. "It feels like shit."

He chuckled. "Again you aren't really seeing it as it really is."

"Maybe so," she conceded. "They did tell me that I was due for another round of surgery, which would fix more of it," she shared. "But, after losing Sam, … I just don't have the heart anymore."

Nobody had anything to say to that, and she knew that every time she brought up the child, it was hard on them too because they were all expecting children, and nobody wanted to think about anything ever happening to their children.

She muttered. "I'm sorry."

"Don't be," Calum replied. "We live in a world where we understand death very well, and we have healers around us, some who even deal with death in a way we didn't think was possible. Then suddenly we're all pregnant and all waiting on our families with hope and joy. Yet we're very aware that there are no guarantees in life. You have every right to be angry, hurt, and upset. … However, it can't interfere with the mission we're doing here because every one of us wants to make it back home again, and that's a nonnegotiable aspect to this job," he explained, looking at her in the rearview mirror. "We all want to ensure that we get back home, to be with our families and to be fathers."

She nodded. "I probably shouldn't have even contacted you. It would have been easier, and then you would have been safe."

"We're safe right now anyway," Calum declared cheerfully. "You forget that this is the work we do. What I was trying to say and did so badly is that we don't want to end up in a position where you don't follow orders, where you don't do something that you're told to do, or where you explain something to us and then do the opposite, all because you're hung up on your own hang-ups," he stated, "and *that* ends up getting us all killed."

"Yeah, I agree with that. We don't want you going rogue on us," Rick said stiffly.

"Jesus, why didn't you just say that to begin with?" she muttered, rolling her eyes. "I wouldn't do that anyway—at least not knowingly."

"But it's the *unknowing* part that's hard to control," Calum pointed out, with a nod. "You might not want to do it or have that as a plan, but it's pretty easy for things to happen unexpectedly to you in the moment."

"*Great.* So, what are you saying then? You pretty much just want me to sit back, shut up, stay out of the way, and do what I'm told?" Calum burst out laughing, and that made her grin too. "Your laughter is very infectious," she noted. "Thank you for that."

He shook his head. "My laughter is just laughter. It's not the domineering force in my world, and it's definitely not a part of Rick's, in case you haven't noticed. Yet, when you have a sense of humor, it really helps to keep things in perspective. Plus, you're pretty much right-on. That's exactly what we want from you. Thus, when you get intel from your energy readings or whatever and know where we should be going, then you tell us—and tell us as soon as possible—so we have time to get where we need to be."

"All I can tell you right now is that we're ultimately going the wrong way. I've got threads going in the completely opposite direction."

"Good to know. Meanwhile we'll change vehicles, and we'll cross the border in the dark. Hopefully tonight."

She didn't say anything to that but sat back, as they pulled up to a small farmhouse, and it appeared to be completely empty. As Janna got out, she looked around, but

Calum placed a finger against his lips and hustled her inside. Once inside, she noted the place was vacant. Maybe squatting in an empty house was part of the plan. She didn't know. The guys seemed to be completely unconcerned.

As she went to open her mouth, Calum tapped his lips again, and she realized this would be a *silence only* deal. At least until they checked it out.

He pulled out some small hand-held tool and quickly walked through the place. When he came back, he looked at her and smiled. "No bugs, so it's safe to talk."

She opened her jaw as if to say something, then snapped it shut. "I never thought of that."

"No, and you don't have to. You don't have to worry about those things because we do."

She just nodded.

"The best thing you can do now is get some sleep. We have some rough provisions, sandwiches for tonight, but, if you can crash first, then at least you'll get the maximum amount of sleep because we'll be on foot tomorrow."

"Right," she replied. "So, we're crossing the border in the dark?"

"We are. At a couple places around here, we can get across pretty easily."

She nodded, then walked into the room where her backpack was. Pulling out her jacket, she lay down and curled up with it over her shoulders, though it was hard to fall asleep because of what she'd just been told. She had a chance to sleep, but availing herself of the opportunity was so not her thing. Closing off her mind and shutting things down was a whole different story, but, hey, if she could do this, she was all for it. And she didn't dare complain about the food or the lack of warmth, about nothing. She was heading for Royal, and that's all she cared about.

The fact that she even cared revealed a lot about where her heart was at. She sent out messages to him, telling him to stay close, to take it easy, that she was coming and bringing help. And, with that thought uppermost in her mind, she slowly sank into a deep sleep.

ROYAL WOKE UP feeling confused and weary, and he could swear some other energy was in this room. He didn't know what the hell was going on, but it fascinated him. It was as if lights were dancing around the cold cell. When the door opened suddenly, he looked up from where he sat on his bed to see his jailer walk in with a tray of food of some kind, but he knew it would be the same crap as always.

He didn't say a word. The jailer walked over to Bruce and placed one finger against his throat to check if he was alive, then shrugged and turned, as he walked out without saying a word.

Once he was gone, again Royal waited for a few minutes to ensure the jailer wasn't standing on the other side listening in. Then he got up and walked over to Bruce. "You awake?"

"No," he muttered. "Not if I'm in the same damn place again."

"You are, but there's food."

Bruce opened his eyes and looked at him. "Please tell me it's a T-bone steak with a baked potato and a whole pile of hot veggies. Maybe some garlic bread."

Royal grinned. "Glad you have a sense of humor still, but, nope, it's the same old gruel."

At that, Bruce slammed his eyes closed. "I guess I really

have to though, don't I? That way we are strong enough to walk to the firing squad and all."

"Hey, stay the course," Royal muttered. "I think you're starting to look a little better."

At that, Bruce frowned at him, and then, with wonder in his tone, while looking confused as hell, he said, "I think I feel a little better, but how is that a good thing? Now I'm more aware of all this, all so I get shot next week?" He shook his head. "God, this is such a freaking nightmare. I just want it to be over with."

"You and me both, but I don't want it over by us dying," Royal stated, "and that appears to be the way you're thinking."

"No, I'm not thinking, and that's the problem. I've been in here so damn long that there is no room for thought anymore. I'm just slammed up tight between a rock and a hard place, but I do appreciate the fact that you're here," he shared, looking over at Royal. "I really do." Then he sat up, frowning. "You know what? I am feeling better." Bruce looked around the room. "How is that even possible?"

"I don't know," Royal admitted cautiously. "You are looking okay though."

"And yet I could swear I was in a coma before, and the days were just running in this endless loop."

"I can agree with that," Royal noted. He wasn't at all sure what was happening, but it was almost as if somebody had found him and was sending energy or doing something to help, for both him and Bruce. Royal just didn't know how the hell such a thing was even possible. Yet Bruce appeared to be getting stronger by the minute.

When they finished eating the gruel, both of them just shoveling it down, knowing they needed the sustenance,

Bruce looked back at him and yawned. "I think I'll crash again."

"You do that," Royal said. "And, when you wake up next time, you should be even stronger."

"Stronger for what though? Strong enough so I can walk out there on my own power and take a bullet?" he muttered. "God help us." With that depressing comment, Bruce crashed again, dropping off to sleep so fast it was eerie, as Royal watched it happen.

Royal looked around the room, not at all sure what was going on, but, when he saw the light dancing about again, he muttered, "I don't know who you are, but thank you for helping Bruce," he whispered.

The light pulsed, as if suddenly aware, and it zoomed to his side, zapping into him with a force that surprised him, but he let it, as a tingling sensation ran along his arms and moved throughout his body. It was pumping him up and making him feel way better. He didn't have a clue how or why, but he was grateful nonetheless.

CHAPTER 3

JANNA WOKE UP to somebody shaking her. She silently sat up in bed.

Calum said urgently, "We're leaving in twenty minutes. Come get a bite to eat."

She got up, used the facilities, then headed to the kitchen, where she was handed a couple big, thick sandwiches. Her eyebrows shot up at the amount. She ate what she could, then handed back the rest, which the two men quickly scarfed down. A sandwich that big was obviously so far out of her league in terms of quantity, but she ate what she could and was full. A couple granola bars were set before her, which she stuffed into her pocket.

With everything packed up, and her backpack on her back, they slowly moved out into the darkness. She had hiking boots on her feet, and good ones, but she hadn't had a whole lot of time to break them in. Even now as she moved at their side, she tested her feet, hoping they could get a good share of the way before she got blisters. She had Band-Aids with her, just in case, but it would still be better *not* to have that problem in an op like this.

She kept up with the men as they moved silently through the darkness. When they came to a series of overgrown brush hedges and what appeared to be a large waterpipe, they traipsed inside, getting their feet thoroughly wet, but it led them through a dark and wet drainage ditch. When they came back out on the other side, they quickly moved into the brush again, out of sight of anyone.

Rick caught up with her, having been in the last position, and he whispered, "We're in Russia now."

She nodded and pointed to the south. "We need to go that way." He didn't say anything but nodded, yet kept going the same way they had been. She didn't have any choice but to follow. Now in Russia, they all remained silent. Yet somehow she felt that Rick and Calum were communicating anyway. She had no way of knowing for sure, except that some weird energy buzzed around her at various moments.

All of a sudden Calum stopped, turned, and whispered to Rick, "The women say they found both of them."

Janna gasped. "*Both* of them? So, somebody is with Royal then."

He nodded and whispered, keeping his voice very low, "And you were right. They're to the south of us, but that's all they can pick up. They're funneling as much energy that way as they can. I'm being told that the other person is quite sick, and that'll hamper our rescue."

"Absolutely," Janna stated, "because rescuing only one is not an option."

The men turned to stare at her.

She jutted out her jaw. "You don't know which one is sicker, and it could be Royal." The men just continued to stare at her. Almost abashed, she added, "Besides, we won't leave anybody behind, will we?"

The men shared a look, didn't say a word, and kept on walking.

She didn't know whether they were in agreement or not,

but she would raise Cain if they thought they would come all this way just to leave somebody else to suffer, as Royal had been suffering.

When they had walked for about thirty minutes, she got an odd mixture of feelings. "I can almost feel him."

"But they're not that close," Calum noted in surprise.

"I know. That's why I'm not sure what's going on. Whatever it is, that connection between us is much, much stronger now." She frowned as she looked at the men.

"Most likely it's Clary and Cara."

"What do you mean?" Janna asked, as she tried to keep up with them.

"The twins have opened up healing pathways, which means that their combined energy is flowing to Royal and his buddy, probably at a much stronger rate. You should know better than we do, but you're probably tapping into that energy too."

She wasn't even sure what to say to that.

"I'm not sure exactly what all you were doing with the government," Calum admitted, studying her, "but surely you understand that energy flows and highlights or strengthens all the other energy work going on around it, right?"

"Nothing like that ever came up in any of the testing that I was involved in," she shared, "but it makes sense."

"See if you can contact him," Calum suggested. "The twins used your energy to get there. So, if you could open a door and communicate with Royal, that would help a lot. He should know that we're coming, and we can coordinate with him and make a plan to get him out."

"I'm trying," she replied, "but, in the last while, there hasn't been any change."

"Keep trying," Rick interjected. "You'll find that communication changes and that door will spin open, maybe too fast for you to even see or to do anything about it initially, but then it should be something you can reopen again."

She heard what he was saying, and, even though she didn't quite understand it, she got the gist of it. She was still reeling with the idea that the women healers had used Janna's energy to reach Royal somehow, not to mention working on somebody else in the room with him. Just as she took a couple more steps, a shot rang out around them.

She was thrown to the ground instantly, with Calum whispering in her ear, "Don't move."

SOMETHING HAD SHIFTED, but Royal didn't know what. He paced and stretched in the small room, trying to keep his body limber, not sure what was going on but feeling a surge of excitement. Any change was a good change, at least in this instance. It had nothing to do with the prison, at least as far as he could tell. He walked to the door, and for the first time in a long time tested it, and, when it turned under his hand, he sucked in his breath and carefully poked his head out.

He saw absolutely nothing here but the empty hallway and other shut doors, with rooms probably similar to the one that he was in. He walked over to Bruce and shook him awake.

Bruce looked up at him, bleary-eyed.

"The door's unlocked," Royal whispered, his tone harsh.

Immediately Bruce's gaze narrowed, and he stared at him in shock. "Why?"

Royal shook his head. "I don't know. A trap maybe?"

He shrugged. "Maybe."

"But the latch itself hadn't dropped all the way, so I could open it. It could have been a trick or an oversight, but I don't know. Why now? Why today? What I do know is that we have a couple hours before our jailer is due to return, and his visits have been like clockwork up until now."

Bruce slowly sat up, tested being vertical again, and said, "I don't know how far I can go, dude."

"You can go far enough," Royal declared. "The fact is, you're sitting up, and that is way more than I thought I would ever see out of you."

Bruce looked up at him and smiled. "You're right. I'm not sure what's going on, but I'll take this energy and use it." As they both stood, and Bruce walked slowly to the door, he asked, "Even if we can get out of here, where will we go?"

"It doesn't matter. First off we get the hell out of here." Royal looked over at him and asked, "You were military, weren't you?"

"Navy. Twenty-nine years old and dying in a hole here. You're right. I would much rather get shot while trying to escape then staying in here, waiting to die."

"I'm not planning on getting shot at all," Royal declared.

"Yeah? You'll go find that woman, won't you? She must be one helluva gal to keep her in your mind all this time."

"Yeah, I'll go find her all right," he vowed, with half a smile, "but let's get out of here first."

"Yeah, at least you have a woman to keep in mind while you try to escape," Bruce noted. "Me? I ain't got nobody."

"That's not true. You've got family, right?"

"Now that I do have. You're correct, I've got family," Bruce confirmed.

They took one look at each other and slipped out into the hallway, moving quietly, hoping no other prisoners were stuck inside this clammy, nasty-ass prison. They made it to the end of this hallway and reached the intersection of another hallway, where they stopped and took a look around. They heard a sound, almost as if a TV were playing ahead of them.

Royal looked at Bruce, then slipped forward. Approaching the open doorway, Royal peered around, saw one guard snoring, his feet up on the table in front of him. Royal quickly walked in behind the guard, and, rendering him unconscious, he dropped him silently to the floor.

Bruce came in behind him, sweaty and pale, then nodded. "Do we kill him?"

"No," Royal muttered. "We aren't them."

"No, but they can come after us," Bruce noted, "and I don't want to leave more warm bodies than we have to, who can later catch up to us."

"I get that," Royal replied. "And you have more reason than me, having been here longer, but my vote is no. We don't really have time either." He quickly picked up the guard's weapon, while Bruce checked the guy's pockets, cleaning out money that they would need, plus an ID, even taking his hat and his jacket. With a smile at that fast thinking, Royal nodded in agreement and quickly replaced the guard's clothing for his own. "I'll move him to our cell."

And, with that, he quickly had the guard inside their room, locking him in. Royal returned to find Bruce searching the place. He was now dressed in a uniform as well, having gone through everything and turning up another weapon for him too. Bruce even found food and some coffee on the table in a travel mug. Royal was surprised.

Bruce shrugged. "Hey, we have to survive, so let's grab what we can. I've got all I could find that was edible, plus money and weapons and my own uniform to wear." And with that they headed out the guard's TV room and down the hall to a laundry area. "How come they never used that for us?" Bruce asked.

"Doesn't matter now," Royal muttered. He pointed at another big coat. Bruce grabbed it. Royal felt bolstered having weapons and ammo with them. They headed forward, where the lighting was more abundant. As they went partway down the hall, they saw an exit sign. Heading down another hallway, they quickly walked toward the exit sign, glaring in front of them.

A man called out from behind and asked in Russian, "Hey, you, what are you doing?"

Keeping his voice low, Bruce turned and said something back in Russian.

The other man snorted.

Bruce continued to talk to the other guy, as he walked toward the exit door. They opened it and stepped out, when Bruce called back something else. As soon as they were outside, and the door was closed, he muttered to Royal, "We need to move now."

Royal asked, "What did you say to him?"

"Said I was taking five for a smoke break, and he could fire me if he didn't like it. Then he laughed, and I told him we'd be right back. So, we have five minutes, and then all kinds of shit will happen."

"Got it," Royal muttered. "Let's move."

Holding the weapons in front of them, they moved steadily to an area where parked vehicles were, and they hopped into one. Although they had no keys, Royal bent under the ignition, popped some wires, and quickly hot-wired it. With the vehicle started, he sat up and put it in gear, heading for the now-open gates to the facility. They had almost made it when a shout came from behind them, and the gate started to close.

Royal gunned the vehicle as hard and as fast as he could, squeezing through, just as the gate closed behind them. He looked over at Bruce, grinning. "Now *that* is teamwork."

"Yeah, and now we're in the deep-shit time frame," Bruce replied, his energy fading quickly.

"No, not necessarily. We've got a few minutes head start because of the gate, which they're opening behind us, and then they'll be right on our ass the whole way," Royal noted.

"That ventriloquist stuff was a kid's trick," Bruce shared, "but what we're coming up against now will be a whole different story."

"Yep," Royal agreed, "but you and I both know we can do this. With stage one done, in a way that we never even thought was possible, we can still hope. So, remember that."

"I know," Bruce said, "and now I'm just …"

"I understand. You're exhausted. Close your eyes and rest as much as you can because it'll get ugly up ahead. And we don't have any choice now. We must move, and we must move fast, and we'll ditch this set of wheels as soon as we can too."

"Yeah, well, look at the road around us. Nobody's here. I see nothing, and the terrain outside of this area is heavy and ugly," Bruce pointed out. "We won't just drive along and hope that nobody'll notice. We'll have to outrun them, and, depending on how much gas we even have, that might not be possible either."

"As soon as we run out of gas," Royal noted calmly, "we'll hit the rough terrain on foot, so rest while you can. You've got a little time."

With a snort, Bruce closed his eyes. Sure enough he soon crashed.

Royal still wasn't exactly sure what was going on, but he knew that somebody was helping them by sharing their energy. He called out to the ethers telepathically, *Don't know who you are, but thank you. We're free of the prison, but now we're in for the fight for our lives.*

The only person he ever knew who had this ability was Janna, which he'd heard through the grapevine, not from her directly. Supposedly she had been involved in a government program and had walked, after some huge stink had happened. That explained why she wouldn't even let him talk about governments and the work he did for them. That was one of the reasons why he'd known that he couldn't stay with her because he was so firmly entrenched in that kind of work, which routinely involved governments.

She had also been very clear about not wanting a permanent relationship, but maybe just something short-term. As it turned out, that's exactly what it had been. But he'd never forgotten her, and it had stayed with him for a long time. The fact that her face had been damaged hadn't been a problem for him, but he'd known that it was a big problem for her. She kept telling him to go, to do something else, to be with somebody else, and he couldn't get her to change her mind.

Over the years he'd sent out probes, trying to figure out just what he could possibly want for a future without her, when everything inside him screamed that he needed to spend time with her instead. Yet even attempting to figure it all out was almost impossible. For years and years, he'd thought about her, going back and forth over all of it, that one fated weekend with her, still trying to contact her and yet getting nothing in return.

Every once in a while, he thought he felt a probe from her, recognizing that she was probably thinking about him and trying to contact him, but it was the weirdest thing. He used energy for energy. He didn't know anything about using energy otherwise. She had mentioned that energy could be used in all kinds of ways, but he didn't really understand but one use for energy, and she hadn't been too open about discussing it further. So that had been that. And yet he'd never forgotten her, and even now that's where he was heading. He was going to her.

He had told Bruce as much, in the endless hours they'd had nothing else to do but pass the time by talking, saying that, at some point in time, you realize that what you really wanted in life you had to go after, even if it appeared to be somebody who didn't want anything to do with you. You shouldn't let that discourage you. You had to convince them otherwise. It would be better and easier if it weren't somebody with as many hang-ups as Janna had, but Royal certainly understood where she got them. He knew that love could make so much of it go away, and he was all about trying.

The years had gone by, and then he'd been imprisoned. So the one person who had kept him alive and sane while he had been incarcerated in Russia had been her. Just the thought of being able to return to her, the challenge of finding her again, spending time with her, that was his lifeline. He knew she wouldn't believe him. Why should she?

In all this time, he hadn't bothered to reach out to her, not effectively. Yet now it was all he could think about. Keeping an eye peeled on the road behind him, knowing that the Russians had to be coming fast, as soon as they figured out what was going on, Royal drove at breakneck speeds, trying hard to stay ahead of the craziness that was about to erupt behind them.

Yet nobody was behind them.

He whispered to his sleeping partner, “I don’t get it. Where are they?”

When a voice slammed into his head, he cried out in shock and pain. Immediately the volume turned down, and he heard a calm voice speaking in his brain.

We’re trying to help you. Just keep driving, and drive fast. We’re trying to cover up your tracks.

He didn’t say anything, but he drove faster, not that there was much more that he could pull out of this old set of wheels, but he was doing his damnedest. So, if somebody was out there helping him, well, he was all for it. When he got over his shock a little, he whispered, “Who is this?”

Let’s just say a friend of yours sent us.

“Who?” he asked, his tone sharp. “I don’t have many friends who could do something like this.”

Yeah? Her name is Janna, and she was getting messages for help from you. So she contacted me. I’m Terk, by the way.

Royal’s breath let out in a gush. “*The* Terk?” he asked. “The mysterious man of magic?”

A note of laughter filled his tone, as he responded. *I don’t know anything about* that *Terk. I’m just flesh and blood, but I do have some psychic abilities, and you’re getting a taste of them right now.*

“I’m grateful,” he muttered. “I don’t know what the hell’s happening or how to get the hell out of here, but holy shit, Bruce and I, … we’re so grateful. The execution was set for next week.”

You have to do some things though, Terk added. *You must*

follow instructions very carefully. We have a team coming to you, and I'm running a smokescreen behind you, with the help of some of my people. We can't keep it up, so I'll need you to ditch that vehicle as soon as you find other wheels.

"I don't even know where I am," Royal shared. "We were imprisoned, so I have no idea where we actually are."

And I can't tell you either, Terk noted calmly. *So, just keep driving, and we'll keep doing what we're doing. However, as soon as you find another road or anything that can get you off this main highway, you take it,* he stated, *because we can't keep up the smokescreen forever.*

"Got it," he muttered, and then he hesitated. "Is she okay? Is Janna okay?"

Yes, he replied, his voice getting faint. *She is now, but she's not the person she used to be, and she could really use a friend.*

"I'm always there for her," Royal said.

Maybe you don't know, but she really needed you a while ago but couldn't tell you. And now? … Well, she's injured inside in ways that you won't understand until you've had a chance to catch up. She's in Russia looking for you right now. And, with that, Terk's voice slipped out of Royal's mind.

In Russia right now, looking for me? Royal sat back, still driving at breakneck speeds, with hope in his heart for the first time in a very long while. Yet shock and worry overtook his thoughts, trying to figure out what the hell had happened to Janna. They'd said their goodbyes. He was supposed to call her, and then, out of the blue, Royal had been sent out on another mission almost immediately.

Since Royal and Janna supposedly had a friendship without strings, when he hadn't gotten back for another nine weeks, he'd realized it was probably too late and hadn't called her. Just back from another *government work thing* to avoid discussing with her.

Now he realized that call—or lack of a call—had probably been what was wrong with his life these past eight years. How did one even begin to reconcile that? He'd never met anyone like her. Never, and the woman could communicate with energy, even work with energy. She'd been so unique, … amazingly so. Even the possibility of a long-term relationship seemed to put her off when it came up in their conversations. He hadn't felt as if he could really bring up that topic again, and the door had slammed closed between them.

He didn't have any way to understand it, but that's what it felt like. But now, hell, if she was in Russia for him, … she needed to get the hell out of here. If the Russian government ever found out what she could do, or if they had any idea that she was back and was worth something, they would keep her prisoner until they broke her. And he didn't know for sure just what that would take because the woman he'd known had been stronger than anyone in his life. Yet that wasn't the woman Terk had described.

Being a woman and a prisoner in Russia was a whole different story. The last thing he wanted was for her to fall into Russian hands. All he wanted right now was to get her home, get some peace and quiet between the two of them, and sort everything out.

While he knew that time was a great healer, all he needed was a chance with Janna. A chance to make that phone call that somehow he had screwed up on, by not making it in the first place.

CHAPTER 4

JANNA STAYED FLAT on the ground, as footsteps raced toward her, with Calum half beside her, half on top of her, making sure she didn't move. She heard voices behind them screaming in Russian. She understood enough that the shooters were sure they'd hit somebody and were coming in to check. She didn't move at all. When Calum was roughly picked up and dropped off beside her, and then another set of hands grabbed Janna to see if she was alive, she knew almost instinctively what Calum would do, as soon as they dropped him.

She watched it happen in slow motion as Calum rose up, almost as if a ghost on the wind, and wiped out the man who had reached for them. Meanwhile Rick came out of the shadows and took out the second man. She didn't know what to say, but there was no time to talk, as she was quickly jerked to her feet and told to run. She ran straight ahead, not having any idea where she was supposed to go, but any place was better than staying where she had been.

No more gunfire sounded, and, when she was tackled from behind, she lay flat, hearing Calum say, "Stay still, just don't move." She didn't. She froze, her heart slamming against her chest, her breathing coming out as if heavy diesel exhaust.

Finally it all calmed, and Calum whispered, "Okay,

we're in the clear."

She opened her eyes and whispered back, "How the hell can we be in the clear after that?"

"We took them out," he said, his tone harsh, as her eyes widened. "No, we didn't kill them, but when they wake up, they'll wake up mad and with a headache, and that'll just piss them off. We have to get the hell out of here in a hurry."

And, with that, she was helped to her feet again and noted they were in a forest, hidden for the most part. "We need wheels," she muttered, looking around.

"Yeah, you got some?" Calum quipped.

She looked at him and nodded. "Yeah, some in that barn over there. I just don't know whether they run or not. The energy tells me that mechanical logic, a car, is inside, but I don't know whether it's functional."

He looked at her, then over at Rick, who holstered the additional weapon that he'd garnered and slipped into the barn. When they heard a car start seconds later, Calum looked back at her, both eyebrows raised.

She shrugged. "I have an affinity for things, mechanical things." His astonishment was complete. She added, "Yeah, just don't tell anybody, will ya?"

He snorted at that. "Are you kidding? In the kind of work that we do, that's huge."

"No, it's not," she countered. "I just find some of this stuff, but that doesn't mean I know how to drive it."

But the barn doors opened, and the vehicle came toward them, slow enough that she could tell it was Rick.

He unlocked the door and said, "Get in."

She quickly crawled into the back seat of the vehicle. As the door shut, and they moved forward, she sighed with relief. "Thank God for that," she muttered.

Rick looked at her. "How did you know the car was here?"

She glared at him. "I get it. You don't trust me, but I'm not here to try and kill you. I'm here to try and save Royal."

"Sure," Rick conceded, "but that vehicle was behind closed doors."

"Apparently she has *an affinity*," Calum repeated in a mild tone, "for mechanical things." Rick stared at him, and Calum shrugged, then added, "Look. I'm not arguing the point. I'm just telling you that we have seen some pretty wild and crazy things from energy workers, and, if she can do that, I'm grateful because, right now, we needed the wheels, and we wouldn't have any chance of finding these, particularly in the dark. We wouldn't even have looked inside a barn."

"Probably not," Rick agreed. "We would have just picked up the pace."

"Exactly. Now picking up the pace is one thing, but we're here on the road now, so it's all good."

"It's probably the vehicle owned by one of those guards who just shot at us," she noted.

Calum nodded. "That would make sense. And, if they're smart, they'll wake up from their very long sleep in the cold and realize that their vehicle is gone and come up with some excuse for why they failed at their job," Calum shared.

"And could just simply steal another vehicle from somebody else to keep themselves out of trouble," she noted.

"Don't worry about it," he muttered. "They won't get shot over this."

"Maybe," she muttered, "but they'll certainly throw us to the wolves, won't they?"

"Maybe," he admitted. "I mean, they have to do something to justify their mistake. However, if they're found to be completely incompetent by letting us go or letting us slip away from them, that won't look good on them either."

She didn't say anything to that but settled back. "At the next intersection, take a right," she said.

They didn't say anything but did take the next right. As she sat here, she could sense Royal's energy. "Something shifted," she stated, leaning forward. "Take the next left. He's on the move."

"What do you mean, on the move?"

"I don't know," she snapped. "I'm just saying that Royal is on the move. He's not where he was. I don't know why. I don't know how. Yet he seems to be moving, and fast."

At that, Calum pulled out his phone and quickly called Terk. When the voice came through, albeit full of static, he asked him about Royal. Terk's response was grim.

"Yes, they have escaped. They're on a road about 250 miles from you, heading in your direction. You need to be heading in their direction, which means taking the next left."

As that's exactly what Janna had just said, so both men looked at her, one through the rearview mirror and one by turning in his seat.

She shrugged. "I don't care if you trust me or not, but I won't do anything to hurt Royal, not at this point. I also don't understand what's going on with his energy and the energy of the person beside him," she shared. "That is very suspicious."

Terk replied, "The twins are sending them a lot of energy. The problem with that is, it's wearing down our healers, and they can't keep it up. The young man who's with Royal is quite severely ill, and only because of the twins is he functioning at all."

"*Great.*" Janna groaned. "The healers need to keep that energy for themselves and for their babies."

"They know what they're doing," Terk noted, his tone calm and soothing. "Believe me that I won't let them do anything to hurt the children. Neither will they exert themselves."

"I know," Janna admitted, "but it doesn't always happen quite so easily as you say it does."

He laughed. "As you well know, we can do a lot of things that we never tried to do until we're tasked to do it," he pointed out, "just like you finding that car."

"Yet you know I've had an interest or an ability for mechanical things," she replied. "It doesn't always help though."

"No, it sure doesn't," Terk agreed. "What matters is having the right team in place to do the job."

"I'm not right for your team," she snapped. "You know that. Besides, yours is a government team, so I won't even touch it."

"We're not a government-backed team anymore," Terk reminded her. "You're still thinking with your old history. You need to stop that and move forward in life."

"Right," she murmured. "as if that'll happen."

"It can," he said, "but that really depends on whether you'll let something that's really important to you slip through your fingers again."

At the *again* reference, she glared at the phone. "*Thanks* for that."

"Hey, no point in pulling punches," he muttered. "It's important that everybody knows where everybody stands in an op like this."

She sat back and sighed. "Maybe so, but I don't know

where I stand with Royal, so it doesn't make a helluva lot of difference. I'm doing my best and trying to keep him alive. I don't really know what I'm doing, but I'm sending him as much energy as he can use, but yet I realize the person with him is in bad shape."

"He's in very bad shape. I'm not even certain we'll get him out of there alive. That will be very hard on Royal because he isn't aware how much other people are utilizing their energy to keep his friend alive. At some point in time it may not be enough."

"*Great*, so we're bringing back a corpse."

Silence came on the other end at first. Then Terk responded in a low tone, "Agreed. It is possible. In which case we will drop the body. As you and I both know, that body is not the same as a soul. While the family might want to have his body for closure, we can't risk lives to make it happen. So our focus is to try and get two healthy, two alive males out. Barring that option, getting a live one out is still better than watching them both die in a Russian prison."

And, with that, he was gone.

ROYAL KEPT DRIVING, staring down at the gas gauge, completely aware that he didn't have too much more gas in the tank. As he came upon road signs, he started to smile. "Looks as if civilization may be up ahead."

But there was absolutely no sign of life out of Bruce beside him, and how Royal hated that phrase. Yet every time he tried to call out to him and talk, no response came. He needed a set of wheels that he could steal and jumpstart quickly, then move his friend into, so he could get them out of here. The fact that other people were out there trying to help was incredible, but they were still hundreds of miles apart.

They weren't here, not right now. They weren't able to give him a hand at this moment, and that meant that Royal had to do this himself. A small town was coming up, but, if anybody saw him, regardless of his Soviet uniform, it was still very obvious that he wasn't a local, not one of the maybe fifty people who lived here. *That* was a problem. He couldn't exactly go in and steal a vehicle without people knowing about it, and, if only two vehicles were in front of a store, neither would be a good thing to steal either.

He pulled around to the back of one of the mom-and-pop stores and found a small truck there. He parked the prison rig beside the truck, then got out and moved Bruce over. After hot-wiring the truck and pulling out, moving as fast as he could, Royal was beyond grateful that the tank was at least half full.

Half a tank wouldn't get him as far as he needed it to, but it would get him somewhere. He didn't have enough money to fill up—or at least he didn't think so. Bruce had the money on him, courtesy of the prison guard. Still, Royal didn't know exactly what that would buy when he got to a gas station. He would have to figure it out coming up to the next town or village. Still, he had hit civilization and was thankful for that. As long as he could keep moving, that was a huge help.

He also didn't have a phone. They had taken the first guard's cell, but Royal hadn't had a chance to even log on and see where he was, see if there was a GPS, or see if he could even utilize the phone at all. What he needed was Bruce awake and functioning. He reached over and gave his buddy a shove, but he got no response. Bruce lolled in place, his body moving back and forth with the motion of the car. "Shit," Royal muttered.

The last thing he wanted was to be caught with a dead body, if that's the way this was heading. And, of course, it's the way it had been heading since forever. Whether he could get Bruce out of this nightmare was the question, and it took everybody's assistance to make it happen thus far. Royal just wasn't sure Bruce would make it all the way. Royal called out for Terk. "You still there?"

There was a faint affirmative in his head.

"Do you know where I am or where I'm going? I only have so much gas, and I need a destination to head for."

All he got was *Keep moving. I'll contact you.*

Royal groaned at that but kept driving. When a moan came from beside him, he glanced over to see Bruce looking over at him, pain in his eyes, and his skin almost looked ashen. That worried him. "Hey, you're awake."

Bruce shifted in his seat and looked around. "This is a hell of a lot different."

"Yeah. Do you even remember that?"

"Vaguely," he muttered. "God, I just remembered the prison, and that seemed like forever ago." He shivered inside his heavy coat.

"Hunker in and warm up," Royal ordered him. "We do have some help coming, and I did switch out vehicles and just dragged you in and moved your sorry butt over," he explained, with a snort. "You're welcome."

"Thanks for that," Bruce muttered. "I can't say I would have appreciated being left behind."

"No, we're not doing that. Yet we're not out of danger by a long shot. As far as I know, I got away with this vehicle, but no way to know how far we get until somebody comes up behind us. I want to make another switch if I can, not to mention that this one doesn't have a ton of gas."

"Oh, yeah, gas is important. I don't think we have enough money to buy gas."

"You want to take a look at what you got and see what we have in terms of assets?"

At that, Bruce checked his pockets and nodded. "I have $47 here, so that might buy us something. Food would be nice."

"It would, though I'm not sure our stomachs could handle it," he noted, his tone serious.

At that, Bruce nodded. "I get that. I did find a couple granola bars. Do you think we could handle that?"

"I'm willing to try," Royal replied, staring at the granola bar in Bruce's hand. "Is there just one?"

"No, two."

And, with one each, they quickly opened the packages and started eating. "Also we have cold coffee in this thermos. It was warm, but it's cold now."

"Yes, but it's a liquid, and no doubt we're probably chronically dehydrated."

They split that, amazed at just how much better even that little bit made them feel. As they came up to another small town, he pulled around to the back of another store and cased out the vehicles. Finding an SUV that looked as if it could go the distance, he parked beside it, hopped out, checked the dash, managed to get it going. Fortunately it also had gas.

Since it was fully fueled, he nodded over at Bruce, who made the switch on his own, collapsing inside the car, even as Royal started backing out. "God, we've been awfully lucky so far," Bruce managed to get out.

"Yeah, and I think part of that is due to our friends."

Bruce looked at him in surprise. "What do you mean?"

"I don't know how much of this I believe," Royal began, "but it seems to me that either I'm hallucinating or we have somebody helping us with camouflage." He mentioned Terk's name, watching for a reaction. When Bruce looked at him blankly, Royal explained, "He's the guy who was in that government operation, where their own government turned around and tried to kill his whole team."

Bruce frowned. "I don't think I remember hearing about that."

"Yeah, well, if you were in the navy, you heard about it," Royal stated. "I think the CIA did it or some such unit. God, it was such a nightmare. Everybody was pissed off. It was a classic case of killing our own team to keep them quiet or some bullshit like that," he muttered.

"That sucks," Bruce muttered. "but I may remember something now about a guy named *Terk*. That's not a common name."

"Apparently Terk's got a helluva lot of tricks up his sleeve. Either that or I'm losing my mind."

Bruce shuddered again and sank back against the seat cushion. "While we're on the road again, are you okay if I crash?"

"Yeah, you can crash," Royal said, "but first do you want to see if you can get into that phone?"

"I tried," he muttered, "but it's got a password on it."

"Of course it does. Go ahead and sleep then," Royal suggested. "If you can't get into the phone, I can't tell where we are anyway." And, with that, he took a look at his friend, surprised to see Bruce already out cold. But Royal's own belly was full, and he had another vehicle that had gas, and, so far, they didn't have anybody behind them. So how very lucky they had been.

He was starting to realize that this was a case of far too much good luck, without some otherworldly help. So, he was pretty sure that Terk, whoever this guy was, literally had been helping them. And that went a long way toward making this a hell of a lot brighter day for him. And, with renewed hope, Royal sent out a message to Janna. *Thanks, sweetheart. I don't know where you are, but I hope you're safe. Please stay safe until we can get together, and then we need to talk.*

When a voice came through his head that he recognized, he almost hit the brakes in shock. But it sounded, dammit, just like Janna, as she whispered in his mind.

Royal, just know that I'm trying to get help to you. Stay strong. I know you're hurt. I know you're hurting, but we're getting there. Honest, the cavalry is coming, and, this time, with any luck, it's coming for you and your friend.

CHAPTER 5

JANNA DOZED IN the back of the car, slipping in and out of sleep as the miles droned on. She kept a link in the direction of Royal, but nothing changed, nothing seemed to be any different. When a phone jangled, breaking the long stretch of silence, she shifted in the back seat and sat up to listen.

Calum put it on Speakerphone. "Terk, what's up?" he asked.

"Danger. Get off that main road. Find some place or another way to travel. Royal and his friend are also heading into trouble themselves." And, with that, Terk ended the call.

She sucked in her breath, wanting to ask a million questions, wanting Terk to give them some assurance, to get some assessment that everything would be okay, but she knew from the silence around them that it wasn't to be.

At that, Calum turned and asked her, "You got any direction in mind?"

She stared at him blankly and looked around. "All I can tell you is to go right."

At that, Rick snorted. "What is with you guys? Left, right, left, right, that's about all we ever hear."

She stared at him. "Do you have others who can do this?"

"Yeah, one anyway," he replied, "but, just like you, he's always on the verge of vague."

"I'm not necessarily accustomed to doing this," she shared. "And I'm worried about being wrong."

"We don't have time for being wrong, but neither do we have time for cautious," Calum noted, twisting in his seat to face her. "So, if anything triggers you, we need to hear it immediately because we are making some moves now."

"But we have no place to go. This road only heads in one direction," she cried out.

"It goes to all kinds of places, as all roads do."

She frowned, her mind suddenly glomming onto the problem. "Ditch the car."

Immediately Calum looked over at Rick, but Rick was already pulling the vehicle into a copse of trees and parking. Calum eyed her and asked, "Seriously?"

She nodded. "Get out now." She was already scrambling for the door handle to exit the vehicle. They'd barely made it off the road and into the trees when several other vehicles came from the same direction they had been traveling. These vehicles hit the brakes just as they went past, then squealed and backed up toward them.

"Oh God," she whispered, as she was jolted from her stupor with Rick and Calum pulling her in the direction of the woods around them. No snow was on the ground, thankfully, and they weren't leaving tracks—or, if they were, it wasn't much. Still, Calum and Rick were insistent on getting her deeper and deeper into the trees. She appreciated that they had their heads in the game more than she obviously did. Yet she knew something very similar was happening to Royal.

She was already tired, and her legs were sore, and she

could barely even function as it was, and still they were moving so fast. By the time she was allowed to stop, her legs were beyond shaky, and she collapsed onto the ground, gasping for breath. She looked up at them, about to say something, then stopped because there was no point. No point in arguing, and she didn't have the energy for it.

Calum crouched in front of her. "Hey," he murmured. "Sorry for the speed. I know that wasn't a comfortable pace for you, which is why you're out of breath so badly, but, when we tell you to run, you run."

She gave him a slight nod, as she got her breath back. When she finally felt more in control, she whispered, "Royal's having the same issue coming up."

"Can you warn him?"

She shrugged. "If I wasn't using all my energy to keep myself conscious, I might. I've been sending him messages for days, even before this op began, but I don't know that he's getting them. Hell, I don't know that he's gotten any messages," she admitted, struggling to keep the bitterness from her tone.

"We understand that. Just keep doing what you can."

"Why is it that doesn't ever seem to be enough?" she asked, staring up at them. "How can you keep doing this job without ever knowing anything, without ever having any assurance available to give you a confirmation that what you're doing is right?"

"We do have hope in Terk, who is usually working in the background. Even in his silence, sometimes we just take it all on faith," Calum replied, with a wry smile. "And, when life happens, you do the best to adapt and to stay on your toes, though you don't have much of anything else you can do. We don't like those kinds of cases, but they do happen.

We just listen and keep going. … That's the best any of us can do." With that, he held out a hand to her and added, "Speaking of which, we need to keep going."

She groaned and let him help her get back on her feet again. Still shaky, she looked over at Rick, who appeared not to be affected at all. "I gather you guys are used to running for your lives through woods at the drop of a hat."

Calum shrugged. "We're also *not* sharing our energy, trying to keep somebody else alive." He gave her a pointed look. "And your energy is draining in too many directions."

She stopped and stared at him. "What?"

Calum frowned. "Do you not know that's what you're doing? … An energy that's uncontrolled or not balanced can also be very dangerous. Terk could help you learn more about that," he stated.

Rick walked closer and studied her. "Yeah, she's sending a lot of her energy to Royal." He gave her a hard look. "So, you might be telling us that you don't really care or that it's all just because he's the father of your child, but I can see energy very clearly, and I do understand that you are filled with an awful lot of emotions."

"Sure," she confirmed, "emotions are involved. I told you that. But I have no clarity as to those emotions. It's too confused with everything else that's going on."

"Sure it is," Calum agreed, his tone soothing. "Dealing with layers and layers of trauma and energy is not something you'll sort out overnight."

"And yet it feels as if I should," she murmured, as she stared around at the space she was in. "This is particularly painful for me."

"Yeah, for us too," Rick stated.

She glared at him. "Look. I get it. You've got a problem with me, and I wasn't really trying to cause you any trouble.

I am trying to save Royal, though."

At that, Calum grabbed Rick's arm and hers and addressed them both. "If you two would solve your personal problems and get over it, we would all get through this a lot faster."

Rick stared at her for a long moment and then nodded. "I get that you are a newbie energy worker, but I can't have you holding us back. That's what I've been worried about right from the beginning. You are proving my point, as, even right now, you're holding us back. We're using energy to keep ourselves on our feet, and, as much as I appreciate the fact that you're using your energy to help keep Royal on his feet, you're slowing us down. You need to understand that your energy flow is not enough to do both."

"Yet energy is universal," she snapped.

He gave her a crooked smile. "Exactly. So why aren't you using the energy around you then?"

She blinked. "You don't understand. … When I told you that I had an affinity for things metallic or mechanical, I meant it."

Calum, who had walked ahead a few feet, stopped, pivoted back to her, and asked, "Do you mean that you can draw energy from all things metallic or mechanical?"

She nodded slowly. "Yes, that's how I usually get my energy. … Even surrounded by Mother Nature here, I'm one of those weirdos who gets energy from inanimate objects. So, while you guys have your energy flowing through you at a regular pace, I was doing much better in the vehicle because I could get energy from that."

The men just stared at her, as if she were not from here.

Finally Calum shared, "Energy is everywhere around you, and you have absolutely no need to only get your energy from inanimate objects."

She stared at him furiously. "You do know that we're all different, right? If I could get it easily from other areas, I would. It's just that my energy source comes as second nature from metallic objects. Otherwise I work much harder at it."

The two men looked at each other, and Rick chuckled. "The more we're in this industry, the more we realize we don't know everything. Now, nothing here's inanimate, so you'll just have to plow through," he told Janna. "Maybe you could cut lover boy's energy a little bit and let the others sustain him, if they can. Then let's get you back into a vehicle as soon as we can, where at least we know that we won't lose you on this journey."

ROYAL HATED TO say it, but he felt his energy flagging. He looked over at Bruce, who was still out. Yet energy was flowing through the vehicle, so he knew that something was going on. Royal just wished some of it was for him. Almost immediately some energy surged in his direction, giving him a jolt.

He sat up straighter in the vehicle. "Thanks for that," he muttered aloud, with a big smile. "I'm not sure who you are and what's going on here, but …" Just then a sudden instinct slammed into him. He would call it an instinct, but it was almost a voice, something dark and cloudy.

Get off the road now.

He didn't question it for a moment and swerved the vehicle off the road and into a bank of trees, but he didn't have a whole lot of places where he could hide. Knowing that he had to make do, and, with his instincts still screaming at him to get out of the vehicle, he exited and raced around to Bruce's side. He bent down and groaned, knowing that the energy expenditure to do this would be horrific, but he had no choice.

Picking up his friend, he tossed him over his shoulder, grateful in a weird way that Bruce had lost so much weight. In Royal's also weakened state, that was likely the only reason Royal was even capable of carrying the load, he figured, as he slipped deeper into the trees. Once they were safely out of sight amid the brush and trees, he sat quietly, knowing no way he could run, alone or with Bruce. So the best that he could do was try and make a stand here. In his rush to save himself and Bruce, he had left the two guns and ammo behind in the car.

So he really had no way to defend himself. He looked around to see if anything in the forest might help him.

A tree stood off to the side that had branches low enough that he could possibly get up in it, but he couldn't leave Bruce exposed on the ground. He looked for a way to cover and hide his friend, which should work as long as Bruce stayed unconscious. Royal found quite a lot of brush and downed branches on the ground, and he quickly laid Bruce in a good spot, brought over a bunch of brush from the area, then piled it up and around him, leaving his airways clear and free. Then hearing sounds and voices coming his direction, Royal jumped up to the lowest limb of the tree, then scooted on up as high as he could go.

Up here, he started pouring as much Mother Nature energy into his system as he could, but it was slow and tedious because he himself was worn down, exhausted, needing energy, food, and rest. Yet none of that was happening anytime soon.

He almost laughed at that because the other thing that wasn't happening was his becoming a prisoner again. Not again. Not now. Not ever. He hunkered down on the branch, wrapping what little energy he had around him, as if a blanket of camouflage—something he knew other people could do, but he'd never had a chance to even practice or try out such a skill himself. Yet he knew the energy was here for him. It was all around him, but helping Bruce had drained a lot of Royal's own supply. If he could just rest here long enough to recoup some energy, he would be fine.

At least that was the thought. And, with that, he sank into half a stupor, opening every portal he could to pull as much energy as possible from the trees and his surroundings, even as he heard sounds of men approaching in the distance. He shuddered and sank deeper, willing Bruce to stay quiet. This would be a terrible time for him to wake up. Almost as if he had put the thought into his buddy's mind, the brushes below him stirred. Royal tried to send a message to Bruce, but it wasn't getting anywhere.

He watched with almost a fatalistic sense of despair as Bruce shifted enough that the brush, or at least a part of it, fell away, leaving him exposed. Now Royal had two options. He could climb down and cover Bruce back up again, or he could stay up here and hope for the best. But he also knew that, if Bruce was found, so was he. And, with that thought, slowly, stealthily, he climbed down from the tree, until he was on the ground, moving the brush around to hide Bruce better.

As he slipped around behind the tree to try and crawl back up again, a man called out to freeze. Seconds later, the butt end of a rifle was slammed into his kidney. With his heart sinking, he realized he'd been found.

CHAPTER 6

CALUM AND RICK and Janna were still on foot, moving forward, heading toward some point in the distant future, and she could only tell them to keep walking in one direction, when suddenly she froze and cried out, "No, no, no, no."

They turned to her. "What?" Calum asked.

Rick asked, hard and glaring, "Now what?"

"They've been found," she muttered, tears in her eyes. "Royal and Bruce." She frowned at that. "Wait, I don't know who Bruce is, but that's the name."

"Fine. Who found them?"

She shrugged. "I don't know. All I'm getting is an SOS."

"*Great.*" Rick turned to face Calum. "You getting anything?"

"No. Let me check in." Almost immediately he blitzed out.

She frowned at the two of them. "Can you guys just go in and out all the time?"

"Yes, at least if someone is available to let us do that," Rick replied, as he studied her. "Yet you have a lot of abilities. I'm surprised you haven't developed them."

She stared at him. "You develop your skills in groups. You know that, right?"

"You also develop in isolation," he reminded her, "because, when it's necessary, that's when our innovation rises."

"Maybe," she muttered, "but I don't think that kind of isolation was quite what I had been reaching for."

He nodded, not saying anything, which she appreciated. She understood that he hadn't been terribly impressed with her arrival, though it wasn't even so much her arrival as the fact that she had insisted on coming along. She was slowing them down, and that continued to be an issue.

At that point Calum stepped forward. "Yes, Royal's in a tussle at the moment," he shared. "They found him, but they didn't find Bruce."

"But they are together," she stated, looking at him. "If they found one, surely the other one is not far behind."

"I'm not sure, but Royal's been taken. Anyway he's collapsed. Cara and Clary are working on it, but they're not terribly hopeful."

She glared at him, dropped cross-legged onto the ground, and started sending energy to him. Urgent forceful energy. When she got a response, tired and slow, she realized just how physically depleted Royal was, as he could manage only a few words.

Can't help. Weak. Need energy.

She stepped back out and stared at the men, tears in her eyes. "He's too weak. … All I could see around him was trees, darkness, and an energy that I couldn't see because it was on the other side of him."

At that, Calum stepped forward, grabbed her by the shoulders, and looked her in the eye. "You can *see*?"

She looked up at him and nodded. "Yes. I don't see anything else, but I can see in front of him."

"So you see from inside his body, looking outward, or do you see him yourself?"

She blinked, trying to sort through the question.

"As in, are you seeing from his perspective, or can you see everything, like from above them or whatever?"

"I'm seeing through his eyes, but he's not staring at the people who caught him, so I can't see them."

"Fine," Calum said, with a nod. "Even that is huge."

"It's not enough," she wailed. "I can't … I can't help him."

"Sure you can. Have him turn to face the other men, and we'll see if we can do anything from here."

Blinking at that, she instructed Royal to turn around, and, when he did so, falling against the tree trunk, she felt the tears collecting in her eyes again. "He is so weak," she whispered. "He can barely stand."

"That's fine," Calum said. "What is he seeing?"

"A single man in a Russian uniform, holding a rifle on him, some sort of a … long rifle. I don't know what it is."

"Move on," Rick said in a clipped tone. "Is this other man alone?"

She studied the area through Royal's eyes and nodded. "It doesn't appear that anybody else is there. I can see a vehicle at the road, but I don't know whether it is Royal or this guy's."

"That's fine too," Calum replied. "Now, can you transmit any energy to him?"

She frowned at him. "I have been," she said cautiously. "With him so weak, all I am doing is trying to keep him alive."

"Right. Well, this is a bit dicey, but, if we connect to you, and you connect to him, do you think you can direct the energy as we want it?"

She gave a snort. "I haven't been able to do anything you

guys have asked me to do yet, at least not in any recognizable form," she muttered, yet her determination kicked in. "However, I can try."

"That's all we ask," Calum noted. "Depending on what this other man wants and is planning on doing, and whether the Russians want Royal back alive or not, this could be his only option."

And, with that, Calum and Rick shared a look and then stepped forward and put their hands on her. "Now, follow these instructions carefully."

And what followed next was one of the most bizarre scenarios Janna had ever experienced in her life, much less participated in. Still, as she followed their instructions, she stepped even more fully into Royal's world, telling him not to worry and to stay calm. With the two men directing her, she took over Royal's limbs. It was like watching a martial artist working from the outside, yet being connected on the inside in some weird way.

Janna didn't even physically connect Royal's body with the other man, yet energy came off Royal's arms. Then the gunman was on the ground and unconscious. Frowning, Janna stepped back out and asked them, "What the hell was that?"

Rick and Calum both smiled. "Don't worry about it. Tell Royal to get to his attacker's vehicle, which I hope is military-issued, so that he and Bruce can get through more blockades. Plus, Royal must take the man's weapon."

She groaned at that, worried about Royal's energy levels, yet she immediately connected to Royal. *I know this will sound strange, but get that man's gun and any other things on him, then get Bruce to that man's car.* And, for the first time, she heard Royal reply, his voice gaining in strength.

I've already cleaned out his pockets, got the keys, the weapon, ammo, and his coat. I've done one trip to the car with all the contraband. Now we're on to the second trip. I don't know what you just did or who you even are. You sound just like Janna, but it can't be. Then came a series of grunts and groans, as he slowly lifted Bruce. *If you've got any energy to help me get Bruce to the vehicle, I could really use it now.*

Immediately she reached out with both hands, grabbing Rick and Calum, firing energy Royal's way. As soon as she started doing that, she could no longer see from Royal's eyes. She frowned, but it was as if the overwhelming flow of energy blocked off her third-eye sight, almost blinding her. She still heard him grunting with every step, and she felt the force jarring his body, the bones grating against each other as the muscles struggled to hold his frame upright under the added weight of Bruce.

And then finally Royal whispered, "I'm at the car. I think I'm okay now." Then, without any warning, the energy between them detached.

She dropped the men's hands, staring down at hers in awe. "He's in the vehicle," she whispered. "Bruce is with him. He stripped down the guard, took everything he could utilize, got his buddy into the guard's car, and now they're driving again. They're in a military vehicle."

"Okay, that's good. As long as he's dressed in a coat and wearing the Russian uniform, that will help them a lot," Calum declared, with a nod. "I'm already liking this guy."

She smiled. "You would like him. He's all about honor and ethics and doing right for the country," she murmured. "It's just … he's had a pretty rough year, or more maybe. I guess I don't really know."

"Yep. All of us have our own pretty-rough years to go

through," Calum noted. "Now we need to do our job and go meet him. Do you have an idea where they are? Or is there any chance you can direct us toward them?"

She looked at him in surprise. "If I had a map, I might be able to tell you where he is and where he's heading."

Rick snorted, pulled out his phone, and brought up a map of the area where they were, the GPS telling them what restaurants were close by.

She stared at it in delight. "I don't think of technology in the same way you guys do," she murmured.

Rick quickly scrolled through, finding the closest area to where they were, and pointed. "This is us. Now where are they?"

Frowning, she slipped the screen side to side trying to find exactly where they were, but the energy messages were coming in incomplete bursts, uncoordinated, or maybe it was just her. When she finally glommed onto one area, she widened the scope so it was more distant, and she said, "They're in here. I just don't know exactly where."

Rick took the phone from her and stated, "That's still a couple hundred miles."

"Sure, but it's not a couple thousand," she noted.

He agreed. "Let's get moving. We'll head in that direction. When we get there, I'm presuming you can give us some better details." The men took off at a good clip, fast-walking.

"I hope so," she muttered, already trying to keep up with them, "but I can't guarantee it."

"We came here based on what you said earlier, so I hope so," Calum replied cheerfully. "So far everything's working. Let's not do anything to destroy that confidence and just keep our hopes up."

She snorted. "Yeah. I don't know what the hell's working because I still don't know what I'm doing, and whatever I'm doing seems to take everybody else's help," she admitted. "I've never worked with anybody ..." And then she stopped. "Well, in many, many years I haven't. I've been pretty much alone, and I think that's part of the problem."

Calum nodded and headed deeper into the woods. "It is the problem. You put up walls. You put up boundaries, and then nobody can get across them. They don't know why things are breaking up or breaking apart, but it's mostly because you set up these boundaries to keep people out of your space. It keeps you safe, keeps you from getting hurt again, yet it also stops you from living a full life because you live inside these walls that are supposedly there to protect you. In reality, they're not doing anything but keeping you more sequestered. In a way, you are a prisoner of your own making," Calum described, his tone gentle. "So, when this is all over, you might want to work on that."

She blinked at him. "Yet I feel like ..." She stared off far ahead.

Calum frowned at her. "You feel like what?"

"As if you guys are dragging down my walls, and I don't have a choice."

He snorted. "We're not dragging down your walls, but necessity is. What it comes down to is this. You have no choice. Those walls come down, and it is critical that we work together."

Rick snorted. "*You* are actually allowing the walls to come down, but, in any other circumstance, you wouldn't allow it," Rick grumbled at her side. "So, probably, from your point of view, it feels as if we're not giving you a choice, and we're dragging you forward, one way or the other. But remember when you were told that you wouldn't like this trip? Part of that warning was because those walls will come down. We can't function properly if you're hiding things, and we can't tell if you're hiding things because you're behind some damn mental wall that we can't work with."

She tried to digest that as they kept walking, but she noticed that this time she wasn't tired. "How come I'm not so tired now?" she asked suspiciously.

Calum looked back at her and smiled. "When you give energy, you receive energy," he explained. "So the more you help others, the more you get help in return." She stared at him, and he nodded. "So, with everything you do to help Royal, in your mind, you're draining your energy. However, if you allow the energy to function the way it's intended, it's replenishing your energy as well. Everything is give and take in life, but it's very much so when it comes to energy." He smiled. "So, the more you help Royal, that circuit completes itself, so you can turn around and receive the same benefit. You don't do it to receive, but, when it comes to something like this, it's a universal law that giving also means getting."

ROYAL WASN'T SURE how long he could keep going like this, but he drove steadily. With this *weirdness* benefiting them, he could only hope that these people working in the background might get him and Bruce out of this mess. When he came up to a blockade, he glanced at Bruce beside him and noted he was propped up, snoozing. Royal shifted Bruce's head, so he appeared to just be resting.

With the weapon at his side, Royal drew near and prepared to stop, but the guards just waved him on through.

Royal lifted a hand and carried on. Now that was far better than he could have hoped for. Filled with so much uncertainty, he had been afraid but surprise, surprise. With a heavy sigh of relief, he checked out the blockade behind him in the rearview mirror. The two men talked naturally, not interested in him.

When he was out of sight and not likely to raise any alarms, he picked up his speed until he was going as fast as he could. He had no idea if they even had speed limits out here, and he really didn't give a crap right now. If anybody tried to stop him, he would just barrel through, yet grateful that he didn't have to yet.

Hearing a sound beside him, he looked over to see Bruce's eyes open, staring at him, somewhat dazed. There was a sweaty look to his face, as if he were waking up from a fever. "Hey, Bruce. How you doing?" he asked.

Bruce blinked several times owlishly. "We're still alive?"

Such surprise filled Bruce's words that Royal had to laugh. "Yeah, I'm nearly as surprised as you are," he admitted. "We've done freaking awesome things to get this far."

Bruce just stared at him, completely shocked. "Wow," he muttered. "Not what I expected." He shifted slowly, wincing, his body ravaged by a lack of food and months of torture. "Will we survive this?"

"That's the plan. We do have some people helping us out, but from a distance."

"Hey, anybody who even knows about us and cares enough to help," Bruce noted, "they've got my gratitude forever."

"You and me both," Royal agreed. "Now we're heading down this road, and I really don't know where it goes. I'm hoping we can get some directions as to how to get out of here," he shared. "We just passed a blockade, and I think they were probably looking for us, their escaped prisoners, but they waved us through, since we are dressed in Russian uniforms. You were sleeping in the front seat, so you missed out on all the fun," Royal teased. "With any luck we'll get the same reception farther down."

"Man," Bruce muttered, as he looked out and around. "Not that I feel good, but, for the first time, I don't feel absolutely horrible."

Royal laughed at that. "I'm not at all against that either. I don't even know if any of our stolen money remains with us, the money that we took from the guards, but we need to buy gas and food soon."

Bruce sat in a mild stupor and replied, "Even the thought of food isn't making me sick. I'm so hungry, yet I'm past hungry."

"You had a granola bar a few hours ago."

Bruce frowned. "Are we in another vehicle or am I dreaming that?"

Royal laughed. "Yep, some guy was following us. I had to stash you under some shrubbery in the woods when we were attacked again," Royal explained, "Getting your sorry carcass back to his vehicle—now ours—wasn't easy either."

At that, Bruce looked at him in shock. "Seriously?" Royal quickly filled Bruce in on all that had gone on while he had been out cold. "Good God," Bruce muttered. "Why didn't you just leave me behind?"

"That's never happening," Royal declared, his tone hardening. "Hell, we survived a Russian prison. No way we can't survive our own escape. I'm not giving up now."

"You know that, if it ever comes to that, … you need to do that, right?" he asked, looking over at Royal, his tone sad.

"I mean, only so much we can do sometimes."

"Yet, so far, I haven't found that limit," he muttered. "So don't even say that shit. If I'm pushing to keep you alive, you need to push too."

Bruce laughed and then stopped. "Wow, that was actual laughter."

"It was. Now I'm not sure how you're feeling and what you might need, but tell me, and we'll sort it out. Otherwise I propose we continue to drive, and hopefully we're heading for a border to get out of this godforsaken country."

"Right. We don't have a phone, do we?"

"We do, but you couldn't get into it earlier."

"I'm feeling better now, so let me take another look." And, with that, he checked his pockets, pulled out the phone that they had taken off the first guard and then sat back. Almost fifteen minutes later he gave a hard sigh. "No, I'm still not getting into it."

"That's fine. It doesn't matter. We'll just continue as we have been. A phone would help because it would give us some idea of where we are, but, other than that, we're definitely heading west."

Within five minutes of him saying that, they passed a road sign telling him what city they were heading toward. He looked over and smiled. "Now at least we know where we are. How's your geography?"

"It sucks," Bruce said. "I mean, it wouldn't be so bad except my brain's not firing properly."

"Right. So, if my geography isn't too bad, I figure we're about three to four hours from a border, from the Polish border."

"Is it that far?" he asked, with a groan. "That means we'll stop for fuel at least once."

"Not necessarily. We do have a fair bit in the tank that we're still working on," Royal noted. "Don't forget. We changed vehicles, and this one's pretty full up. I figure we'll stop at some point in time. I'll need a bathroom break if nothing else."

"You okay with a bush?"

"Damn right I'm okay with a bush. I would rather take a piss on the side of the road than in civilization and end up being back in these assholes' hands again." With that, Royal pulled off to the side of the road and looked around, grateful that nobody was around. "Come on. Pee break."

And they got out, both relieving themselves on the side of the road. With that done, Bruce stretched. "I don't know what's happening, but I almost feel decent."

"Don't sing too loudly right now about that, or you might jinx it. Yet you do look much better."

"I hope so. Anyway, let's get going."

They got back into the vehicle, and Royal kept driving.

"How did you get away from the other guy?" Bruce finally asked curiously.

"It was the weirdest thing, and I'm not sure I have an answer for you. Not a logical answer." Royal glanced over at Bruce. "Did you ever have anything to do with Terk's particular field?"

"You mean, all that paranormal stuff?"

"Yeah."

Bruce shrugged. "I've always had a pretty strong gut instinct but not a whole lot other than that. Although my buddies used to … they used to laugh because sometimes I had the trick of traffic lights always turning green, so I didn't have to stop. I never waited in lines, and there were always empty parking spots waiting for me," he shared, with a laugh. "I'm wondering if that shit is what got me in trouble with the Russians to begin with because, among our group, it was a well-known joke. Sometimes people would fight over riding with me, so they wouldn't be slowed down by traffic lights. But you never know. Still, that doesn't make any sense as to why I was kidnapped."

"It kind of does because that's also why I thought I was kidnapped," Royal shared. "Except that I do some of that energy work, like what Terk is known for. Not that it's helped me at all, or maybe it has somehow. I don't know," he said, "but I'm just grateful that I'm not there in that prison any longer. The guards there never asked me about any of those kinds of skills though. Did they ask you?" Royal turned to face Bruce.

Bruce shook his head. "No, they didn't. They joked about it once in a while, and I just looked at them as if I had no clue what they were talking about. Honestly, I really didn't have a clue what they were talking about most of the time." Bruce yawned. "They were just being complete assholes."

Royal nodded. "We were dealing with one prison, whereas another prison may very well have had a different plan, all because somebody explained it to them. In fact, I was in another prison first, and those guards there did ask me all kinds of woo-woo questions." He snorted. "Did you ever see such shitty communication the way it was with these last guards?"

Bruce shook his head. "No, and yet I'm grateful. It's probably because of their crappy communication that we're even alive. If they had any idea that you could do some of that energy stuff or connect with people who could do that stuff, we never would have gotten out of there. But then again, we also wouldn't have been shot come next Wednesday either." Bruce sucked in his breath. "It really would happen, wouldn't it?"

"It really would. Whether they would have gone through with it, I don't know, but I would never trust them not to."

"I did hear them joking, talking about it, in my nightmares," Bruce muttered.

"Yeah. Last time I saw one of the guards, he mentioned something about you not even making it to the firing line next week, wondering why they were even bothering to bring you food. He thought it was a waste of resources, and they just should let you die."

Bruce stared at him for a long time and then nodded. "And something about that is rattling around in my subconscious. You have no idea how grateful I am that we're out here and that, … well, that you didn't leave me behind."

"Not my style," Royal snapped, his tone hard. "Now you have to do your job and fight to stay alive because I don't know what we've got coming our way."

Bruce nodded. "Let's get the hell out of here, get across the border somewhere, and maybe we can pull in some favors and get us out of here."

"Honest to God, even if we can't, I hate to say it, but I have no problem working in order to get out of here. I have some friends I can roust up, but I think the government has pretty-well forsaken us."

"Ya think?" Bruce quipped, his voice breaking. "Though I don't even know that I can blame them for this. It's just a shit deal all around. Sometimes when you get caught, you know ahead of time that absolutely nobody is coming to bail you out. We go into some of these jobs with that threat in our minds."

"I know," Royal agreed. "I was in a similar scenario before."

"Right, so you know exactly what I'm talking about."

"Unfortunately I do. Sometimes it's just the way it is, but, hey, we're free, and we're staying that way."

"You and me both. Now if there was just some food." Bruce eyed him hopefully.

Royal could only shake his head. "I think we're out of food. If I get a chance to pull in somewhere, maybe we have enough cash that we can buy something."

It wasn't long before they hit a small town and stopped at a grocery store and walked inside, just keeping to themselves, not being friendly, which was probably expected of real Russian military men. They got a couple sandwiches, some fruit, chunks of cheese, and other quick snacks. They paid with the bit of money they had collected, grateful that it was enough, and were quickly on the road again.

With Bruce munching away beside him, Royal drove. "That food will go a long way to improving our situation."

"Yeah, you're not kidding," Bruce said, suddenly stopping. "Before I have another nap, who the hell is Janna?"

Royal looked over at him and glared. "You know who Janna is."

"The chick you were thinking about getting in touch with again?"

"Yeah, why?"

"I don't know. I just keep hearing her in my head."

Royal froze. "Seriously?"

He nodded. "That and some other woman, but I don't know who that is. It's such a weird thing. I don't even know your friend, but it seems, … or feels as if, she's been there for a while."

"Yeah, maybe," Royal muttered, not sure what else to say. "Could also be some hallucinations."

"She should be *your* hallucination, not mine," Bruce pointed out. "I don't have a partner."

"Maybe you don't have a partner, but that doesn't mean that your mind will listen to anything you try to tell it."

"I won't argue with that," Bruce conceded, as he shifted and curled up against the door again. "Anyway, when you talk to her, say hi for me. Pretty sure she's been saying hi to me the whole time." And, with that, he closed his eyes and fell asleep.

Royal was left wondering just what the hell was going on and what was Janna up to … and how much could she even do. He'd heard her in his head too, but, … but was it her or was it some hallucination? He had assumed this was all about his own imagination. Then again he didn't know. However, she had been there. It had to have been her in his head when that fight in the forest was going on. It had been so strange and so surreal that even now he couldn't put it down to reality. When someone knocked on a door in his head, he wondered if that was real too. Then he shook his head, just as the guard's phone beside him started to ring.

He picked it up while keeping one eye on the road, as he moved his finger across to answer it, wondering if it would unlock, yet it wouldn't. He tried several zigzags across the phone, when suddenly somebody came through the phone anyway, and he heard Janna's voice.

"Hey, it's me. Can you hear me?"

"Yes, hell yes, I can," he cried out. "What the hell? Where are you? How did you … I don't even know this number." He was fumbling with his words.

"We're about one hundred miles from you," she said,

"and we're closing the gap. If I thought there was a place that you could hole up and stay, I would tell you to go there, but I'm not sure there is such a place."

"We just left a town after picking up some food. I'm just … Honestly, I'm just nonstop driving."

"We're tracking you, not that it's the easiest thing to do," she shared, "but just be sure to keep a low profile and know that we're on the way."

"Yeah, but you're still quite a long way away," he said.

"Only about an hour according to the men I'm with."

"Who are these men?"

"They're part of Terk's team," she replied, "but I don't know if that means anything to you."

"It does, if it's the same Terk who used to work for the CIA. I do know about him and his team."

"It is, although they've gone private now."

"We should all be private rather than trusting in these governments," he declared. "No, that's not fair. … I knew going in that they wouldn't have my back if something went wrong, and yet it was just a typical job. I wasn't really expecting to get sidelined."

"Let's not have that discussion," she replied, her tone hard. "You know how I feel about the government anyway."

"I do know," he agreed, his tone soft as memories flooded him. "I don't know how you got involved in this, but I'm damn grateful."

"I got involved because you've been calling me," she stated, her tone sad. "For the longest time, I didn't even know how to help or what to do, and I even tried to shut you out. I'm sorry for that"—yet not sounding all that sorry—"and obviously you've been through much worse because of it. If only I could have listened earlier …"

He blinked at that several times. "But I wasn't calling you."

"You were, yet you just may not have been aware of it," she noted, equally calmly. "Anyway, that's not a discussion for today. I've been trying hard to get through to you but finally just decided to try the phone beside you."

"How did you know I had a phone beside me? How did you unlock it?"

"I didn't unlock it. It's just that mechanical things and I get along very well."

"Jesus," Royal muttered. "How come I didn't know anything about that?"

"We weren't together long enough for any of that to come out."

"And yet we had a helluva bond."

"We had a hell of a weekend. Did that create a bond? Maybe, I don't know."

He snorted. "Hey, you're the one who set the rules with *no relationship* being one of them," he reminded her. "I was trying to go along with that."

"And yet you were supposed to call me," she stated, her tone equally hard. "That didn't work out too well either, did it?"

"No, because I headed out for another mission, and then, when I got back, I just didn't know what to say. I did try to call and never got through, so I figured that you were pissed off or something."

"Yeah, and that was the part I never understood." Then she groaned and added, "At the moment, it's just pointless to talk about it. I'm sure I'm as much to blame for that."

"I knew that you never wanted anything permanent, so I was willing to give you some space, but I was really hoping to see you afterward too. Then so much time had passed at that point …"

"This isn't the time or place for our personal issues," she said. "It's draining my energy, so I'll sign off. Keep driving straight. If you come to an intersection and don't know where to go, I'll try to give you a nudge in the correct direction."

"Good. What then? After this, I hope we'll have a talk, a long talk, because I didn't know you could do any of this. Our bond was unbelievable as it was, but all this too?"

"That's partly why I walked away from the government way back when. I just couldn't deal with what they wanted of me. They knew some of what I could do and pressured me to do so much more."

"Right, so this all goes back to that. Shit," he muttered. "I wish I'd known."

"Wouldn't have changed anything," she said. "You've been to hell and back, and I have been too but for a completely different reason."

"You had already been to hell and back because of what that asshole did to your face."

"True, though I'd managed to make peace with that, more or less, but my life has gotten a whole lot worse since then."

"Then we're *really* going to talk," he declared, "because you could have called on me at any time, and I would have been there for you."

"Maybe. But I got stubborn and proud, and then my whole world fell apart, and I didn't have time for any of it anyway. Plus, explanations seemed to be even harder to figure out. So, just as you didn't contact me, I didn't contact you. Anyway, I'm signing off for now."

And, with that, she ended the call.

CHAPTER 7

JANNA STARED OUT around her, trying to orient herself. The guys had stolen another car thankfully, so they were no longer on foot. They had reached some unknown town of indeterminate size. She stared at her hands, wondering at the foolishness that had kept her and Royal apart when it wasn't needed. Royal was right. She'd been the one so adamant about no strings attached, no relationships. She was testing to see whether it was even worth trying for a relationship or whether it would destroy her inside and out, depending on the person involved. She should have trusted that Royal wasn't that kind of person, but she hadn't, and she'd let him get away.

Even though she'd tried, she'd only made half-assed efforts to contact him. As she sat here thinking about it, she realized she could have done a lot more, but she hadn't because it was easier not to. Now she considered all the time that they'd wasted, and all the pain she'd been through alone, feeling angry, upset, and yet …

Her train of thought was tossed around as the car picked up speed and suddenly took a sharp corner up ahead. She was tossed to the side, just as rapid gunfire shattered the back windshield all around her. They continued to drive forward, the guys screaming at her from the front seat, telling her to stay down. She wanted to tell them she wasn't an idiot after all, but it was foolish to do anything but curl up in a tight ball and hope that the shooting would stop, and fast.

Why would someone even be after them? Then again, maybe it wasn't about the op at all. Maybe it was just that they were riding in a stolen car. She stayed down and out of sight, as the vehicle kept driving faster and faster, taking corners so quickly she was afraid the vehicle would flip. She heard Calum calling back to her, telling her to hold on.

She did as she was told, as they went around another sharp corner. She swore to God two of the tires lifted off the roadway, her heart beating out of her chest. Thankfully the car landed on all four tires again and kept on going. She had never experienced anything like this, and the last thing she wanted was to be involved in some race that would end up getting them killed. Still, she had been the one to insist that she must come along with these guys, so she could hardly be complaining about that now.

After a series of hard turns, they hit some rough terrain. She couldn't look out, but she figured they were crossing a field or something. She noted that very soon they would probably make a run for it on foot. Unfortunately she was not ready to do that, after their earlier trek into the forest. She closed her eyes and reached out mentally, seeking more info on their current situation. As soon as she did, she connected to a whole bunch of other vehicles up ahead.

She leaned forward and cried out, "More vehicles are up ahead that we can grab, if we can safely stop and get out of this one."

Almost immediately they made another series of turns, and the vehicle came to a hard stop. Doors were thrown open, and, before she knew it, she was being dragged out.

"Where?" Rick asked.

She pointed to the left, and he took off running, leaving her with Calum.

"You okay?" Calum asked, looking at her worriedly.

"I'm fine," she murmured breathlessly, as she tried to keep up with Calum. Rick was about to head the wrong way, so she called out, "Take a left."

He immediately veered left.

When she smiled, Calum eyed her curiously. "Your reaction's a little off. I wasn't expecting to see you smiling right now."

She nodded. "The circumstances suck, but the fact Rick followed my instructions instead of scowling and asking for confirmation first is almost comical."

Calum smiled. "And as long as it all works, he will likely continue to do so. The minute that something doesn't go the way you want it to go, then believe me that Rick will question everything again."

"Right. Of course, the information is only as good as long as the information is good."

He smiled. "We don't have any choice about that either. Just think about it."

"No, I won't," she said, with a wave of her hand. "Vehicles are there, and he can take one. I just don't know what else could be there."

"Meaning?"

"I just see machinery, lots of metal, and that can be both good and bad."

"It could be a junkyard, and maybe they aren't even drivable," he noted, frowning at her.

"Or it could be a dealer or somebody hoarding, or maybe they're a collector. I don't know."

They heard a vehicle start up, just as they entered a huge

Quonset-looking building. As a vehicle raced toward them, they stopped. Confirming Rick was the driver, she quickly got into the back seat again. He didn't even need to bark at her. Rick didn't say a word, but, as he headed out, she told him, "Turn right."

He turned right, and they disappeared into whatever traffic was around them.

She asked, "Did you guys even get a chance to see who was shooting at us?"

"It was a military jeep," Rick shared, "and we must avoid every one of those that we can."

"Except that's also what Royal is driving," she replied. "That's how they got out of a roadblock. They took a military rig, and that's what they've kept to since."

"That's a pretty smart move. If you can reach out and find one of those for us," Rick suggested, "I would be happy to make that switch myself."

"I'll let you know," she muttered. She closed her eyes and settled back. The energy of war machines was very different than that of, say, a cruiser that would only be taken out on a Sunday drive, never to be touched by rain, never touched by wind blowing hard against the paint job. So she had to pick and choose between the energies.

After about twenty minutes of steady driving, she leaned forward and said, "A military rig is up ahead. It's empty, but I don't know why. I don't even know if it drives. I'm just telling you."

"Good enough," Rick noted. He slowed as they approached, and instead of him hopping out, Calum did, then walked around the military rig, checked it out, hopped inside, and turned it on.

She smiled. "You guys are pretty good at hot-wiring

those things, aren't you?"

"It's pretty easy to do, which works out nicely for us," Rick noted, "so yeah."

They made the switch into the military rig, and they took off again, this time with Calum driving. Rick looked back at her. "Anything else to add?"

"No, not right now." She shrugged. "All I can tell you is that Royal and Bruce are coming toward us, and we're heading toward them. So, at some point in time, we can't miss them."

"Can you judge how long it will be or how far away they are?" Rick asked.

She frowned and closed her eyes, shifting her head, trying to check internally for the length of that cord between them. "Maybe thirty minutes or so?"

Rick nodded. "In that case, connect with them soon, so that either they pull off on the side of the road, and we come upon them—or vice versa. Somehow we have to figure out how to recognize who each other are."

"Right," she agreed. "Drive on now, because otherwise we'll have company very soon."

With that, Calum picked up the speed and raced off into the night.

ROYAL DROVE STEADILY, surprised at the level of awareness he was still managing, even though he was exhausted. It was almost as if he had passed exhaustion into some zone of hyper-productivity. Maybe that didn't make any sense or wasn't even possible, but it was the best he could do to explain it.

He kept driving, wondering how far away everybody was and how they were supposed to find each other, when suddenly a voice slammed into his brain and yelled, *Stop!*

He hit the brakes hard, almost throwing Bruce against the dash. Royal swept out his arm, stopping Bruce, then swore. Royal eased forward again slowly, parking on the side of the road. He looked around, not sure who had spoken to him, but hoping it was the good guys. At this point, he was almost dulled to anything else. When another vehicle approached from the front, he stiffened and picked up the weapon, knowing that trusting anybody right now had the ability to take him and Bruce both out within the next few seconds, and Royal had made it easy for them.

He slipped out of the vehicle, closed the door, and stepped behind it, his gun at the ready. The other vehicle pulled up, facing him on the same side of the road and shut off their engine. Now in the silence, Royal waited as the two vehicles faced each other, then suddenly the back door opened up, and a woman raced forward.

She called out, "Royal, put down the gun. It's me."

He stared, slowly walking forward, placing the weapon on the hood of the vehicle. As she flew toward him, he opened his arms, and she threw herself into them. He was slammed hard against the vehicle and groaned at the impact.

She tried to withdraw, but he held her close and whispered, "That's okay. It's, … it's just so damn good to see you." His arms clenched tightly around her, and he held her as if he would never let her go. He realized that she was hanging on just as tightly.

She then backed up to clasp both sides of his face with her hands. "My God, Royal, I thought we would never find you."

He dropped his forehead to rest on hers and whispered, "I didn't even know anybody was looking for me."

She smiled, tears in her eyes, as she nodded. "Yeah, I was looking, and I have been for a while. But we've got you now."

Then Royal noted the two men coming toward them. Their energy was strong; Royal could tell just from the way they walked. They were both fit, healthy, and a hell of a lot stronger than Royal currently was, and yet he sensed no threat from them. Still, he pulled her up to his side defensively.

She chuckled. "They're with me, remember?"

He nodded slowly. "I remember, but it hasn't exactly been an easy trip so far." At that, one of the men stepped forward, and Royal could see him better.

"I'm Calum," he greeted Royal. "And that's Rick. Janna's led us on quite the dance to get to you."

"Who are you?" Royal asked. "And why would she even call you?"

"We work with Terk," Calum explained, as if expecting that name to mean something.

And it did. Yet Royal didn't understand why it related to these people. "How did she get you guys to come out here and find me? How did you even know?"

"According to her, you've been calling for her, and she hasn't been able to get you out of her mind, so she reached out to Terk. About that same time, the CIA called Terk, willing to hire us to get you back. We'd already agreed to do the job for Janna, so it's basically a two for one."

"Right." Royal frowned. "The government."

Such a wealth of disbelief filled his tone that Calum smiled. "I hear you, and that's part of our problem too. We don't really like working with our government—especially the CIA, after what they did to us—but they do pay well. So, it covered the cost of getting you guys out of here, even though Janna was willing to pay for it.'

Royal turned and looked at her in surprise.

She shrugged. "Hey, I'm not kidding. All I heard was you calling for me. And no matter how much I would like to continue this discussion, we need to get moving."

"I can't leave my friend behind."

"We weren't planning on it."

Calum looked at their vehicle and asked, "How much gas do you have?"

Royal shrugged. "Enough, depending on how far we're going."

"We need the most gas that we can get. So I'll siphon our gas and put it into your vehicle, since yours is bigger," he explained. "So let Bruce just sleep."

While Royal watched the other men take care of everything, Royal remembered being as strong, healthy, and vibrant as they were. It just … seemed so long ago. He looked down at her, still in disbelief. "I can't believe that just because you thought I was calling you, … you came after me." His voice was choked with emotion and wonder.

"It's been a pretty tough few years," she muttered. "We have a lot to talk about."

"Yeah, you're not kidding. How about changing that *no relationship* rule while we're at it?"

She looked up at him and smiled. "Yeah, I pretty much regretted that soon after you left."

"Ya think?" he quipped, shaking his head. "God, when I count up how much time we wasted."

"And yet you may not want anything to do with me,

when you, … when you hear the truth," she shared. "I don't know that I deserve anything more either," she muttered.

Just then the men called out, "Let's go," and Royal realized their conversation was done. He got into the vehicle, now in the back seat with Bruce and Janna, while the two other men were in the front seat, taking over the driving. Royal collapsed against the seat, hating to feel relieved, yet pretty-damn hard not to be.

He looked down as she wrapped her hands around his and just held them close. He shook his head, still not believing it, when a sound came from the other side of him. He looked over to Bruce. "Hey, Bruce, wake up," he muttered.

His friend opened his eyes and stared at him. "Oh shit, did they get us? Are we captives again?"

"No, we're safe," Royal replied. "We hooked up with the rescue group. So, in theory, we're better off than we were."

"In theory?" Bruce tried hard to process that, but he was struggling.

Immediately Janna turned to Bruce, "It's okay, Bruce. Go back to sleep. Hopefully, by the next time you wake up, we'll be out of this country and in much better shape."

"Hopefully," he noted. "I don't have a whole lot of hope for much anymore. I'm just too tired of all this."

"Sleep," she whispered and gently ran her hand over his, patting it gently. "Just get some rest."

He closed his eyes and dropped off again.

She looked over at Royal, concern on her face.

"I know," Royal said. "Bruce should have been dead a dozen times over. I'm not sure how either of us keep surviving."

"The will to live is pretty impressive," she murmured.

"Plus, you guys have been getting some additional help." She eyed him, curious to see if he understood.

"I know we have been," Royal stated. "I don't really understand what we did to deserve it, but I'm grateful."

"I'm not sure *deserving it* has anything to do with this," Janna pointed out. "Nobody should go through what you and Bruce have experienced."

Royal chuckled. "And yet, just because we're free, it doesn't stop the governments, both American and Russian, from doing it to other people."

"I know," she whispered. "That's something I struggle with too. I can't go out after everybody. This rescue op has pretty well wiped me out, physically and emotionally and energetically. I'm afraid I've not been very helpful to these guys."

"You shouldn't have to be," Royal declared. "Terk's team should be very well trained for a mission like this."

"That we are," Calum agreed, turning to look at him from the front seat. "But we also have special tactics that we utilize in these cases, and she's been very helpful along that line, especially in tracking you down."

"I'm grateful for the help," Royal said, "and, yeah, if the government's willing to pay, charge them to the hilt because it's their fault I'm in this scenario to begin with."

Calum asked, "So, what were you thinking when you accepted that assignment? You knew it wouldn't necessarily end well, and you knew you weren't likely to be getting any help at the end of the day."

"I knew it was a risk. I breathed a huge sigh of relief when the mission was completed, and we left everything on good terms. I'd been debriefed and was ready to leave. Then the next thing I knew, I was a prisoner and being tortured.

At that first prison, the guards were looking for information on all kinds of shit that I couldn't possibly have any connection to," he explained.

"I think it was just a fishing expedition or the standard questions they asked everybody in prison. … Maybe I was there and conveniently American, so they were using me to apply pressure on our government, just to get a few of their own released in exchange for me. Then it all went downhill from there. I was eventually moved to another prison, where they never asked us anything. They just worked their psyops on us, telling us weekly that we would be executed *next week.* I never saw a hint of daylight after that for months. That's got to be one of the worst things, at least for me anyway. I really missed it and even now can't quite get enough of it."

Janna sighed. "Daylight is essential for the soul, and that would also explain some of how you regressed physically," she noted, looking up at him. "We will definitely get lots of sun, daylight, and vitamin D into you pretty soon."

"I was beginning to really doubt that we would make it. Our execution date kept getting pushed back, so we never really knew what to expect, and so many times I didn't believe we would survive until then. We were slated for execution again next week, though for the longest time we didn't believe them. We've been slated for that time and time again, and we just figured it was another threat and kept hoping that the US government would work to free us. But then we heard them talking among themselves that our executions were scheduled for Wednesday of next week and that keeping Bruce alive was a waste, since he would just die soon anyway."

She nodded. "Terk heard that date as well and thought it must have been serious enough that it got the CIA to take action to fund a rescue attempt. And here you are. You and Bruce are safe now."

"No, we're not," he argued, looking over at her with a knowing smile. "Not until we're out of the reach of the Russians. Not until Bruce and I are not quite so depleted and worn down that we can't take care of ourselves. That's likely to take several months."

"And that's okay," she replied. "You can have months to recuperate, so no rush now."

Frowning, he pulled something shiny out of her hair. "Glass?" he asked, with a raised eyebrow.

She winced. "Yeah, we've been shot at a couple times."

He nodded. "Right, so we're hardly out of danger yet, are we?"

"Maybe not, but we should be soon," she stated. "The best thing for you right now would be to get some sleep. Why don't you take a break and rest while you can?"

He looked at her, then at the men, and realized for the first time that he could let his guard down a bit. He could relax, just as long as he trusted the people he was with.

She smiled and squeezed his hand. "You can trust them, Royal. They came here to get you, after all." When he hesitated, she shook her head. "We don't know what's coming, so, just as they're forever telling me, we need to be prepared, and that means getting as much rest as we can, whenever we can."

He smiled and shook his head. "Whoever would have thought that military wisdom would be coming out of your mouth."

"That's because we didn't really know each other," she said.

"No, but I wanted to," he murmured.

"Yeah, and there were times that I really missed you too," she admitted. "As I've already mentioned, we have a lot to talk about."

"And some of it I don't really understand," he shared.

"I know, but this isn't the time or the place."

He looked at her steadily for a moment and then nodded and closed his eyes. Letting his head fall back against the seat, he quickly drifted off to sleep.

CHAPTER 8

"ROYAL'S STILL ASLEEP," Janna told Calum and Rick, almost an hour later. "They both are."

"They're both in rough shape," Calum said. "You need to be prepared for a protracted and slow recovery, particularly after a long period of incarceration like that."

"I know," she agreed. "I need to get him back to my place, where I can keep him safe. I didn't want to say anything, but he looks terrible, so thin and pale. He used to look much more like the two of you."

"They've definitely been starved. It's not at all unusual in those situations," Calum explained. "I know that Royal does energy work, but is a newbie, so you might want to talk to Terk about getting him some healing assistance."

"Right." She nodded. "I can help, and I can pay for that too."

"You need to talk to Terk about it first because I'm not sure how that works. You're not that far away from Terk's headquarters, are you?"

"No, I'm only just up the road from you guys. Imagine my surprise when I realized you'd moved that close."

"Right. We weren't looking at the neighbors, before Terk bought the place," Calum shared. "We were looking at the location from a logistics point of view."

"Logistics?" she asked, with a laugh. "You just wanted a

castle."

He laughed. "You could be right. I admit that, once everybody saw the place, it was pretty well a done deal."

"I looked at that castle as well," she shared, "but it was far too big for me."

"Good, because it's perfect for us. I'm so glad it was there, ready and waiting when we got around to needing our own place."

"You should have got around to it a long time ago," she declared. "The government will twist you up and screw you over if they get a chance. It would have been good to get out before all that happened to your team."

"Yeah, but we didn't. Now we decide what jobs we take, and we charge them for the work we do. A lot."

She chuckled. "I really like that idea too." She gave Calum a satisfied smile. "I like that you get some control over what you do and don't take on. And that they're paying much more than the pittance they paid us to do the same job."

"Don't worry about that now," Calum suggested. "You could use some rest yourself."

"How far from the border are we?"

"We crossed the border a little bit ago," Calum replied calmly. "It was one of the unmanned border crossings, and it's nighttime, and nobody gives a crap. This is all pretty well wide open country anyway. You'll see the signs changed to Polish, and hopefully we're now heading toward an airstrip. We're just waiting for the logistics to get us to the correct location."

"If we can come up with a motel that's safe, we should all hole up for a day or two," Rick offered, "because it might take our team a bit to make the rest of the arrangements."

"Definitely motels are up ahead," she stated, looking far off in distance. "Is that a problem?"

"No, not necessarily." Rick looked over at Calum.

Calum looked up from his phone and added, "I've just located one now." He punched the address into the GPS on his phone. "We should stop at least to get food, maybe a shower, regroup, and see what we might need to get these guys out of the country and to Terk's castle in England. I doubt Royal and Bruce have any papers, and that'll be our next issue. We may have to smuggle them into England as well."

"I don't care what we do," Janna admitted, "but, if the US government is helping, can't they help with that too?"

"Maybe for Royal, but that doesn't mean they'll be very happy about us bringing Bruce in."

She stared at him and then sank back. "See? That's the part about not liking governments. I really, really don't get how can they pick and choose *people* like that."

"We have leverage in this case," Calum pointed out, "so I don't think it'll be a problem, but it might take a little longer."

While she didn't want to hear that, it did make a certain amount of sense. From there on, they drove on about another hour before they pulled up in front of a large motel.

She stared up at it and grimaced. "As much as I want to go in there and have a hot shower, a good night's sleep, and some real food, it terrifies me to think that it's a trap."

"It's not a trap, at least we don't think so." Calum turned and looked at her. "Are you getting anything like that?"

She shook her head. "No, although I really don't pick up on human issues very much," she said, "which is why it was such a shock that this guy got into my head and stayed there. So, I don't really sense betrayal or bad situations the way you guys probably do."

"Doesn't matter whether you do or not," Calum noted. "I'll go in and see if we can get a couple rooms. I tried to book online, but their site was down."

Still uneasy, she watched as Calum hopped out and walked into the main office area, and by the time he came back out nearly twenty-five minutes later, she was quite antsy.

But he popped his head into the back window and announced, "Here's the room key card. We've got two adjoining rooms at the back. Rick will drive around, and you guys can get inside." Calum waved his hand down the road. "Fast food is around the corner, so I'll leave you guys with Rick, and I'll go pick up some food."

"Good enough," she said, her stomach growling. "I'll shower first."

He laughed. "Yeah, your bag should be somewhere, but I'm not sure you have any clean clothes left."

She winced. "Even if I have to wear the same thing again, I don't really care. At least I'll be clean for a minute. These guys don't have any clothes at all."

"Yeah, and what they do have makes them look very much like they're part of the Russian army. We'll change that before heading out, but that's all part of the logistics after this. So, sit tight and get settled. I'll be back in a few."

And, with that, Rick drove around to the back. As she got out, she looked down at the two sleeping men and asked, "What do we do with them?"

"You wake up Royal, and I'll carry Bruce," Rick suggested, looking around. "We're on the second floor, and we have outside access, but we really don't want anybody to see us."

She reached in and shook Royal awake.

He stared at her for a moment, clearly confused, then seeing the open door, he stumbled out. "Where are we?" he asked, wrapping his arms around his body.

"We're at a motel. I'm taking you up, and we'll get Bruce into a bed, where we can take a good look and see how bad he is."

Royal nodded. "Both of us have a little bit of stuff in our pockets, whatever we grabbed from the guards. Not sure how much is left."

"Grab everything you can from the back seat of the vehicle," Rick ordered, as he searched the front seat and the floorboard. Janna searched the back seat and floorboard.

Then Rick bent in and scooped up Bruce.

Janna asked Rick, "Will you be okay to carry him?"

"Unfortunately he doesn't weigh much at all, which is another sign of long-term captivity. We'll have quite a job bringing him back to good health. It'll take a lot of time, and he could have some really serious problems that we're not aware of yet, like teetering on organ failure."

"For now, let's keep him alive. That will be a good start," she muttered.

Then urging Royal to keep up with them so they could get him inside, she unlocked the door, popped it open so Rick could walk in with Bruce in his arms. She hurried Royal inside, then followed with a casual glance around, trying to see if anything here was of concern.

Everything appeared to be completely normal, which just made her even more suspicious, but she couldn't do anything about it right now. She closed the door, keeping the world out, for the first time feeling as if maybe, just maybe, they would get through this. She raced over and pulled back the blankets on one bed, so Rick could lay Bruce down. She quickly unlaced the boots on his feet and removed his socks, wincing as she saw festering blisters. And then, with Rick's help, they stripped Bruce of his clothing, down to his underwear, as they checked him over for more injuries and bruises. He was a bone rack, with lots of bruising and some sores, likely from lying on the bed in his prison cell for far too long in one position.

She frowned at Rick. "Did our room come with a first aid kit?"

He shrugged. "If not, I'll go out later and get what we need."

She ran into the bathroom, filling the sink with warm water, then grabbed a washcloth and proceeded to give Bruce a simple bath, while he was stretched out asleep but essentially unconscious. She looked over at Royal. "Are you as bad as he is?"

He shrugged. "Probably. I don't know. I can't say that I'll be too impressive to look at either. It's easy to ignore it when you don't know, but, man, once you accept that you're injured, the pain is a whole lot harder to ignore."

Rick smiled and nodded. "But you're holding up, and that's what counts, so maybe you should have the first shower."

He hesitated. "Yeah, I just don't know."

"Do you need help?" Rick asked, studying him.

Royal had stood upright for so long that he got shaky and unstable. "I need to sit, if that's all right."

That made Janna afraid, and she rushed to his side. "Look. If you can get in the shower, Rick and I can help you," she stated, her tone firm. "We need you clean one way or another, and we need to know the extent of your injuries, especially those we don't even know about. The only way to do that is to strip you down and get you washed up," she muttered.

He hesitated. "I thought you would have one first."

"I'll get one later. We need to look after you guys first," she stated, her tone firm. "Now, come on, into the bathroom with you."

He got up and unsteadily headed into the washroom, while she finished working on Bruce. When he called out, she stepped into the bathroom, Rick behind her, to see Royal completely nude. Her hand went to her mouth as she cried out. It was much worse than either of them imagined.

Royal smiled at her. "Hey, I'm alive, and, thanks to you guys, I might make it." He was a rack of bones. His ribs stuck out everywhere, and his hip bones jutted out prominently.

Janna whispered, "Did they even feed you?"

"No, not really, not very much," he admitted. "Only some weird gruel. I don't think they were all that interested in keeping us alive."

She frowned. "Can you even handle a shower? Would you rather take a bath?" She walked around checking him for injuries, and, sure enough, like Bruce, he had several sores that needed attention as well. She frowned at those. "Those bed sores are not good. We'll fix those right away."

"Sure," Rick replied, "but it'll take time."

She looked over at Rick. "Maybe not as much time as you think."

Rick nodded. "Let me talk to Clary and Cara."

"Come on, Royal," Janna said. "Let's get you under a shower." She turned on the hot water, stripped down herself, and stepped in with him, where she scrubbed his head several times as he sat on the shower seat. Using the soap and shampoo that was here, she quickly scrubbed him from top to bottom, and then did it all over again. By the time she was done, she called out for Rick, as she hid behind the shower curtain. Rick stepped back in and helped lift Royal out, then wrapped him up in towels and escorted him to the nearest empty bed.

She stayed in the shower and scrubbed herself down until she felt clean again. It also gave her an excuse to let the tears flow freely. Just seeing Royal so painfully thin, with open sores, knowing how different he was from the robust man she had known before, just broke her heart. To think that people could be so cruel, when there was absolutely no need for it, and yet those guards had thrived on it. They had thrived on hurting somebody else.

What kind of people were they that they did something like that, not just one day but day after day?

When she finally ran out of tears, she stepped out, put her jeans and T-shirt back on, then washed out her underwear and bra, hanging them on the railing, hoping they would have a chance to dry before she had to put them back on again. Out in the bedroom, she looked over at Rick to see him checking on Bruce.

"How are they?"

"They're both asleep now," he said, turning to look back at her. He nodded approvingly, staring her down. "You look better."

"Yeah, sorry about leaving you to it," she replied. "I had no idea Royal was that bad, so it was pretty upsetting to see the condition he's in."

"Prisoners of war are like that," Rick noted calmly, his

gaze ever watchful. "Are you okay?"

"I am," she said, "though I'm looking forward to having some food coming our way."

"Calum will be here in a few minutes," Rick explained. "I asked him to pick up some medication and ointments and a first aid kit too, so we can start treating all those sores. If you're okay for a few minutes with these guys, I'll have a quick shower."

She nodded. "Oh, sorry, I left my underclothes to dry in there. I'll get them."

"Don't bother. It's fine," he muttered. "No worries. I have a partner. Calum too."

She laughed. "Yeah, good for you. The only man who ever got that close to me is lying here, skin and bones, looking as if he's almost dead," she muttered.

"He's not, and, thanks to you, he'll make it, so remember that." Then with gentle hands he turned her to where Royal was crashed on the bed. "If you've got any energy left to give him, he could use some healing."

Then, with that, he stepped into the bathroom and took a quick shower himself.

ROYAL WOKE WITH a start and stared around the room, blinking at the unfamiliarity of it. The light was at half-mast, and he was on a bed, the softness of it was something that he wanted to exclaim over. He had gotten so used to that hard bare cot.

When he felt someone's energy on him, he whispered, "Where am I?"

"You're on the bed beside Janna," said the man in the

shadows. "You're safe. We met you out on the highway and brought you and Bruce to a motel. We're in Poland. You haven't eaten, but you've been scrubbed head to toe, and your wounds have been treated for the moment," said the same man.

As the man stepped closer, Royal recognized him from the highway and sank back in relief. "God, it seems as if I've been asleep forever."

"We cleaned some of your wounds. Some of those sores were pretty rough too, raw open sores. You're not in good shape, so we ended up giving you some painkillers that knocked you out, but unfortunately we didn't get you any food first."

"Food would be lovely," he replied, as he shifted uneasily. "Wow, getting up will hurt, won't it?"

The man chuckled. "Yes. I'm Rick, by the way. If you can get up and come over to the table, I can get you some food."

Royal slowly stood and made his way to the bathroom first, where he dressed in the casual clothes someone had brought for him, then headed for the table and gingerly sat down. "I didn't think I was that bad."

"Adrenaline and panic keep us going for a long time, but, at some point in time, even that wears down," Rick noted, his gaze focused on Royal. "We'll hole up here for a couple days to see if we can get your strength up a little bit. We need you stronger before we move you two again."

"Will a couple days even do it?" Royal asked, looking over at him. "I feel as if I'll need a year."

"You shouldn't need that long in total, but you'll definitely need a few months. Right now I need you strong enough that, if we must run again, you're capable of keeping up."

"Right. That is a whole different story." His gaze shifted around the room and landed on Bruce. "How is he?" he asked, his voice almost at a whisper.

"He's in worse shape than you, and that's unfortunate because you're not in very good shape at all."

Royal turned to Rick. "I don't feel too bad though."

"Sure, because an awful lot of energy is flowing through your system as energy workers try to help you," he explained. "If you were on your own, using your own energy reserves, you would be flat on your back and probably not capable of moving an inch. That's the danger of giving you too much energy. It makes you cocky, thinking you're okay when, in actual fact, you're way worse off than you thought."

"Okay, that's good to know, and I can see how that would happen," he noted in a calm tone. "Even now I'm ready to go back to bed, but you did mention food."

At that reminder, he was presented with some slabs of bread, plus bottled water.

"Oh my, real food." He noted the meat and cheese, but it was out of his reach.

"Now be careful though," Rick warned him. "You eat too much, too fast, and that could kill you too."

"Right, that's what ended up happening in the Second World War, didn't it? The rescuers were desperate to help people and didn't want to deny them food, but the onslaught of food killed far too many of them."

"Exactly," Rick agreed. "Just like too much water can be bad, like too little water, we have also learned since then that sometimes the kindest thing is to be cruel for a little while."

"You tell me how much to eat then. Otherwise I'll eat everything on this table and probably the table too."

"Yeah, well, you won't get that choice." Royal was given two good slabs of bread, and Rick said, "See how much of this you can get down." When the bread was gone, he was given a bottle of water. "That should be it for now. I suggest you get some more sleep, if you can, and hopefully the next few days will just be a cycle of waking up, eating, then getting more sleep."

"I'm good with that," Royal agreed, as he stared over at the bed. "She really brought you guys to save us, *huh*?"

"She did. She was adamant that she had to be with us. She's the one who came to Terk, even though apparently she's quite the recluse."

"She is, because of her face," Royal noted. "It never mattered to me, but she didn't believe me. I don't think she even had the ability to really believe it could be true. At least not then, but I'm hopeful she's better with it now."

"Honestly, she hasn't mentioned it or dealt with it very much lately. I'm sure other people may notice, but I don't find it all that bad."

"Exactly. I told her that back then, but she was … I think still so hung up on her appearance and thinking that it was way worse. Yet she seems different now."

"She's also been to hell and back, and I know you don't know all the details yet," Rick shared, "and it's not for me to tell you. Just know that she's not the same person, and that's not a good thing either."

"Hell, she's already been to hell and back so many times," Royal said. "The shit she went through over that acid attack and all the surgeries, I can't imagine anything worse."

"Whatever happened to whoever did it, the fan or whatever?"

"Committed suicide not long afterward. I think he was

planning on taking her with him, but she escaped to survive, and the mentally disturbed fan went on to take his own life."

"That's an easier ending than it could have been," Rick replied, then waited in silence for him to finish his water.

Royal drank the bulk of the water and then stumbled his way back to bed. As he sat down, he asked, "Should we wake up Bruce?"

"No, we'll let him sleep right now. I'm monitoring his energy to ensure he's not slipping into unconsciousness, but, come morning, we'll wake him up and get him some food and deal with him then."

"Sounds good." Royal was exhausted from everything that had happened and was way beyond anything he could deal with at present. Yet he felt terrible that he wasn't capable of doing what he needed to do for himself, much less Bruce. Yet here Royal was, willing to crash, because this was his opportunity, until they could get out of here. He closed his eyes and fell into an instant deep sleep.

CHAPTER 9

JANNA WOKE UP in the hospital. Her heart slammed against her chest, her body in shock, as she stared up at the white-robed personnel with masked faces around her. Voices urged her to go back to sleep, to relax, to just fall back under the spell of the drugs, but her mind wouldn't let go. Her mind could see the exact same thing that had happened to her, over and over again.

She shook with the pain of acid hitting her flesh, the bite as it continued to burn into her, and those screams, ... *her* screams. The screams that rose from the pain threatening to overtake her permanently was a broken record, and she could not tune them out.

As she struggled to let them know that she was still in pain and that this had to stop, another voice came from beside her, a calm soothing voice, a voice reaching out, saying, "It's okay. Take it easy. It's all right." She didn't know that voice, yet she did. She just didn't know how.

"It's me," Royal muttered in that same soothing tone.

She whispered, "What's going on?"

"You're having a bad dream, that's all. Just go back to sleep."

She blinked, sure that no way this could be a bad dream. She could see the hospital room. She could feel the bed underneath her. She could sense everything so clearly, not to mention the pain, the pain that just never stopped.

"It's the pain that keeps bringing you back to that nightmare," Royal explained in that same tone, calm and reassuring somehow. "You need to go back to sleep and wake up again. It's over. Let it go. You're fine now."

She gave a broken laugh. "How can it be fine? How can anything ever be normal in my life after this?"

"It will be. I promise you. Normal will happen. It'll take time, though. I won't lie to you. It'll be a *new* normal, but there will be a day when you can see this and can walk away from it. It won't drag you down again."

She didn't believe him, but sleeping was something she could do, and, with that thought, and the drugs maybe tugging her back under, she gratefully sank down into the depths of forgetfulness.

When she surfaced again, it was the same thing, except the hospital scene had changed. She frowned, even now ready to run from this scenario as well, not sure why she was in the hospital, but the pain was still excruciating. Another voice, or maybe the same one, slipped through her mind.

"It's all right. You're fine. Just relax."

She cried out as the pain hit her at a level that she couldn't even begin to deal with, and that same voice whispered, "It's all right. You're fine. Go back under."

And it seemed as if maybe she was given something? She wasn't even sure, but she was grateful to accept whatever it was, as she slowly slipped back under again. By the time she woke for the third time, she was disoriented, confused, and exhausted. She stared around at the weird pink-colored room, surprised to find somebody sitting on the edge of the bed, looking at her.

He smiled. "Hey. Believe it or not, you are awake and

hopefully awake at the right place."

She blinked at that. "What does that mean?" she asked cautiously.

He smiled. "How do you feel?"

"Exhausted, as if I've been running and fighting all night."

"You pretty well have been," he said. "Your nightmares had been pretty horrific."

She stared up at him, feeling the heat wash up around her cheeks. "But they were nightmares, right?" she asked cautiously.

He nodded. "Unless you were expecting them to be anything else."

She shook her head. "No, I'm not expecting them to be anything. All I know is, … life hasn't been terribly easy these last few years, and, under times of stress, I do tend to get nightmares."

"I would definitely say that's going on right now, but you need to know that I'm fine."

She looked at him, recognizing Royal now, realizing that he was sitting up on the bed, looking at her calmly, as if he might be in better shape than she was. She frowned. "How is it that you're okay?"

"I'm not so much okay as I'm holding," he replied, "big difference."

She nodded, but she wasn't sure she understood at all. She looked around the room and said, "I'm not even sure what's going on here right now," she muttered. "Where am I?"

"We stopped at a motel, so that Bruce and I could regain some strength, and we could all get some sleep and a shower."

"Ah, that whole *good night's sleep* thing. Did it work for anybody else?"

He smiled. "It did. Right now Rick is having a nap, and Calum is out getting us food."

"Food would be good," she said cautiously. She shifted, groaning at the pain coursing through her body. "Oh, man, I don't know where all that pain's coming from, but, wow, I feel as if I've run a marathon."

"From what I've heard, you have," he confirmed. "According to the conversations I've had with the guys, you did a lot of running yesterday."

She thought back and then slowly nodded. "I did, and some of it was in pretty rough terrain." She shifted again gingerly, trying to see if it was safe to stand up. "Any chance of coffee?"

"Yep, absolutely." Royal smiled. "I should have figured that would be the first question out of your mouth."

"It's not so much that I'm a coffee nut, but it's *coffee*."

"Take a few minutes then. We should have a little time before Calum gets back."

She nodded and slipped into the bathroom, quickly scrubbed her face and straightened up her hair. Her teeth needed attention but, without a toothbrush, she did the best she could. Then she headed out into the living room. As she walked in, Royal held out a cup of coffee for her. She smiled gratefully. "Thank you, and I'm sorry if I kept you awake."

"I was already awake. I slept solidly for hours, and then Mother Nature forced me to get up and empty my bladder. Then I couldn't get back to sleep. I just stayed up, talking with Calum, checking on Bruce. And, with me up, and you probably surfacing soon, he's gone to roust us some food."

"Thank heavens for that," she said. "We've been pretty

short on supplies for the last while." And then she flushed. "What the hell am I saying?" she muttered. "I'm complaining about granola bars and sandwiches to the guy who has literally been starved. I'm sorry and so embarrassed."

"That's all over with," he noted calmly. "And I'm very grateful for the rescue, believe me." He looked at her curiously. "But I still don't quite understand how it is that you even knew I was in trouble."

"I knew," she reiterated, "and I was really working hard *not* to explain it because explanations are just … awkward."

"Doesn't matter if they're awkward or not," he said. "You're correct in that I was thinking of you a lot. I was really upset and sad at the way we left it, and I figured that, if I ever got free, I would find you and see if we could move forward again, *together*," he shared, with a chuckle. "You were definitely one of the reasons I stayed sane in that nightmare of a hellhole."

She stared at him solemnly and then nodded. "I'm glad you at least had that." She gave him the tiniest of smiles. "My last few years have been pretty rough, and I don't even want to tell you. … Honestly, I think you'll hate my guts."

He stared at her. "Good God, no. I can't imagine what on earth would ever make you think that."

She hesitated, and then in a shaky voice went on, "When you left, you left something behind."

He frowned and looked at her. "What are you talking about?"

"After you left, … I found myself pregnant."

He stared at her and then slowly sank into his seat in shock. "What?"

She nodded. "Obviously this isn't an easy conversation for me. I had been trying to figure out how to get a hold of you for the longest time but didn't succeed because you … weren't that easy to get a hold of."

He stared off into the distance. "I get that. I was off on an overseas mission that ended up not going so well, and I was very late returning, which is also the reason why I wasn't so sure I should contact you either, being so late to call you." He stared at her. "So why are you here?"

"That's part of the problem," she began, "and one of the reasons why I could pick up on anything that you were calling out to me."

"That makes no sense to me because, in theory, that should have only been possible if we were heavily connected somehow. So, … I get that could work if we had a connection that strong, but still it would surprise me."

"We were connected. It was … it was Sam," she said in a rush. "My boy, our … son."

He stared at her in shock, finding the agony in her gaze. "There isn't any good news coming, is there?" he asked warily.

Tears filled her eyes, and she brushed them away impatiently. "He died … when he was just six months old."

His breath came out in a hard *whoosh*, as he stared at her.

She felt the tears crowding her now, choking her throat and blinding her. "I know. … I made a terrible mistake not telling you, not finding a way," she admitted. "How do I even tell you that you had a son and that now he's gone?" she asked. "I couldn't even tell you that I was pregnant."

She shook her head. "I was such a mess and alternated between hating myself for getting into that situation, because I knew I would be an absolutely awful mother given all the trauma I was going through, and …" She just stopped, bowing her head as she tried to regain control.

When he gripped her hands, he spoke softly. "I'm sorry you couldn't get ahold of me. It sounds as if we had … That was probably part of the drive for why I figured we needed to reconnect."

She shrugged. "He was beautiful. He was perfect," she whispered. "I just … I had him for such a short time."

He nodded. "We'll discuss this later in more detail because obviously I want to know more. Are you saying that, because of his birth, we're connected deeper or something?"

"I don't know, but that's all I can figure. Maybe because we had that connection, maybe it was amplified somehow when I heard you calling out."

At that, his eyebrows shot up.

She shrugged. "Yes, I heard you. I tried hard to ignore it because I didn't know what I was supposed to do with it, and then it got worse and worse and worse. Finally I realized you were seriously in trouble. And, for that, I'm really sorry that I didn't recognize it earlier for what it was, that I didn't act sooner. But, even when I did and figured it was something I just couldn't ignore any longer, I didn't really know what to do at first. Then suddenly it came to me, and I reached out to Terk."

At that, Royal glanced around the room. "The fact that you even knew Terk …"

"He had asked me to join his team quite a while ago," she said calmly. "At the time, I had a huge hate on for governments, and he was with the US government still, so my answer was an unequivocal no."

"I'm pretty sure your response was a whole lot stronger than that," he teased, with a wry smile.

"But then, when I realized that you must be in some

serious trouble, I knew I wouldn't rest until I figured out what was going on," she explained, "and Terk was the one who came to mind. And, as it turned out, that was a good thing."

Royal nodded ever-so-slowly. "Absolutely it was a good thing. I'm still shocked, really."

"I know, and I'm not at all surprised. It's … it was a pretty tough go-round, even going in to see him. Because, well, nobody knew about my accident." She reached out a hand, her fingers going up to the scar on her face.

He stared at her steadily. Her face had never bothered him, but she had never really believed that anybody could ignore it.

"Because Terk already knew who I was, I think he accepted what I had to say a whole lot easier than if he hadn't known me already. Anyway, I'd gone to his place to tell them what I knew, and, as it turned out, at the very same time, apparently the US government contacted him, looking for somebody to go in and pull off a rescue."

She looked over in the direction where Bruce slept. "Only afterward did we find out you weren't alone, and, of course, the CIA didn't mention Bruce. So there's no payment for getting him out."

"I'll pay," Royal stated instantly.

She looked over at him and shook her head. "No, you can't do that. I've already promised that I would." He frowned at her, obviously not liking it, and she shrugged. "Deal with it. That was your problem with me before, the fact that I had money. No point in having money if you can't do something good with it. And, in this case, I think saving Bruce's life is definitely worth putting some money into. Not that these guys would have left him behind anyway."

Royal let out his breath slowly and nodded. "Your money was a bit of an issue," he admitted, "but that was stupid on my part. I can pay my own way and don't need your money," he stated, shaking his head with a smile. "And it's not as if you ever threw it in my face, so it was just my ego—something that, believe me, I no longer have a problem with."

She smiled. "No, I'm sure with all that you've been through, that has completely changed your perspective on many things."

"Yeah, you're not kidding," he muttered. "And anything that helps get Bruce back on his feet again"—he gazed once again at the bed where Bruce slept.

"Has anybody seen him this morning? How is he doing?" she asked.

"I checked in on him," Royal replied. "He's holding his own for now. He's in rough shape. If not for Terk's team of healers, I'm sure Bruce would never have made it this far. But then"—Royal took a deep breath—"I don't think I would have either."

She nodded. "I don't have very much affinity for healing with energy, although I do admit I am learning. According to Terk's team, healing is just something that we do automatically, but there are ways to make it happen a lot easier, a lot faster, a lot smoother," she explained, "particularly for other people. So, I'm still learning."

"Good," Royal replied instantly. "I don't know Terk myself, but I've heard good things."

She smiled. "Yeah, everybody's heard things about Terk, but he's still got that mysterious element. Although, since working with his team, I certainly understand a lot more."

"And yet you trusted him?" he asked.

"I did. Anybody who does this energy work, well, it backfires pretty fast if you don't go about it the right way or have the right reason for using it. I also know that he can't *not* do this work because he's as gifted as he is. When I realized that he'd gone private, after the US government tried to take out him and his team, he was definitely somebody I was prepared to deal with. I would have happily paid the whole price to get you back, but the fact that there were two of you to rescue was even more of a concern. Then the fact that the US government had left you behind all this time, that was all I needed."

He smiled. "Oh, so you were just looking for a chance to stick it to the government?"

She grinned. "I might have had a bit of an issue with them."

"Did it have anything to do with your face?"

"Somewhat, but it's definitely not today's conversation."

"As long as it doesn't impact what we're doing here."

"My hatred of the government is something I am working on, not very well and not very fast, but … I am working on it."

"Is it really a hatred?"

"No, it's more about despising those in power," she replied calmly. "Now, something like Terk does, I could see doing work with him and his team. Other than that, I don't know. I very much want to learn more from Clary and Cara, these healers who have helped us so much on this lovely journey," she shared. "And, if I can do anything to help them out, then I would love to do so."

"I think you sell yourself short," Royal noted. "You have so many talents that you don't even allow yourself to be aware of, and you are constantly shortchanging yourself, thinking that you have nothing to offer. And I really think so much of that is because of your face."

"Maybe," she conceded. "You only have to look at the crazy world we're in to see just how people react to my face."

"And yet not everybody does, definitely not me."

"And that was the anomaly I didn't understand," she told him. "It's one of the reasons why I hesitated to contact you because we'd had such an absolutely phenomenal weekend—plus Sam had been the result of that too. It was a miracle conception, as we both used birth control. Still, I could never quite fully understand why you would care or would want anything more to do with me, with my face the way it is."

"You're the one who put that rule in place," he stated. "You're the one who was making sure I didn't cross any lines and start thinking there would be anything more."

"Sure, and that was completely self-protection on my part."

His mouth opened as if he would say something, but then slammed it shut, as he just stared at her.

She shrugged. "I figured if I said that, you would leave or I would leave you, and then you could never hurt me by leaving me."

He stared at her in confusion, as so many emotions crossed his face. "That is a very twisted way of self-defense. Good God." He scrubbed his face. "I'm not sure I've had enough coffee for this."

She burst out laughing. "Yeah, you and me both," she muttered. "But I am glad that I could finally tell you about Samuel."

"I am too. Yet it is devastating to find out after the fact

that he even existed, and I never had a chance to know him, to hold him."

"No, you didn't, but you also didn't get your heart completely broken because of it. Not sure that either way was better. It's just the facts of life."

He didn't say anything but looked at her with that same unfathomable expression that she'd never really understood before.

"That look right there," she murmured, "that's part of the reason."

His eyebrows shot up. "Part of the reason for what?"

"Part of the reason I couldn't understand why you would want anything to do with me."

ROYAL'S BREATH CRASHED outward in a big *swoosh*. Janna's words still reverberated in his heart and soul. To even think that a child had come and gone, and he hadn't even had a chance to meet him was heartbreaking, but to know that she had gone through all that alone, without anybody there for her, broke him even more.

Royal knew that she would have been alone throughout the entire thing because she felt so isolated from the world around her, so lacking in trust after what had happened to her that she didn't have anybody she would trust enough to call on. He got up and walked over to the window again, not even sure he could trust himself to say the right things.

She got up, stepped behind him, and whispered, "I'm so sorry."

He turned and looked at her. "For what?" he asked. "For looking after our son? Even though it was beyond your control to keep him alive? For going through a pregnancy alone, when you couldn't get ahold of me? For dealing with as much of your problems as possible at the time that you could?" he asked gently. "Would I have wished this to have been any other way? Absolutely. But it wasn't, and this is what we have to deal with,"

Royal continued, "Obviously I would have preferred that it had happened in some other completely nonpainful way, and I wish that Samuel hadn't passed on, but he did, and I'm on the other side of this now. I'll obviously take some time to process it all," he noted, "but, in the meantime, we're in a hell of a pickle still, and it would be much better for everybody if we sorted ourselves out."

When she looked at him steadily, he smiled.

"And, no, I don't mean chasing you away or anything else," he spelled out. "You've … you've been incredibly generous and caring to even help me escape in the first place, and it will take me a bit of time to process Samuel's …" And he stumbled over the word. "Samuel's birth and death, but that too is part of the cycle of life, isn't it?"

She let out a slow, deep breath. "I thought you would hate me."

"I don't hate you. I could never hate you. I'm still in shock at the news, and I'll grieve for a child I never had a chance to meet, and that breaks my heart too. I always figured children wouldn't be a part of my life because of the work I did."

She nodded. "I always figured that children wouldn't be a part of my life because of my accident."

He nodded. "I know, … and I've told you this a million times," he said gently, "and I'll tell you a million times more, but your facial scar doesn't matter."

She winced. "Yes, you will have to tell me a million times over," she admitted, "because I get that, in one way, it doesn't matter. Yet it still seems as if it matters."

"No," he argued, "it doesn't matter in the least, and, if I were to finally get just one thing across to you, it's the fact that you're beautiful. You are so beautiful just as you are, and, if anybody's got a problem with your scar, it's *their* problem, not yours."

She let out a snort. "My face became much less of an issue once I realized I had Sam coming, and then after I lost him? … That again put things in perspective in a big way."

"But not in an easy way," Royal whispered. "It wouldn't have been easy at all to come to terms with that."

"No, it wasn't, but it did make me realize my looks just didn't matter in the bigger scheme of things," she shared, with a partial smile. "I'm working on it. I really am, and I've come a long way. The doctors did tell me that I could go back for more surgery, and this time it would make a huge difference, but I just … I'd come to the point where I couldn't do any more."

"If you feel like it, do it, but you don't need to do any more if it just stresses you out," Royal noted. "If you want to do more, that's a whole different story. However, any time and distance you put between the surgeries is always a better thing for you anyway. Time to heal, time to heal properly, not just being anxious for the next surgery to improve another five percent, though that can make a huge difference in some cases."

"You do get that," she said.

"I do. I've watched lots of my friends go through multiple surgeries after coming back from horrific injuries in war," he shared. "Sometimes the surgeries work, and sometimes they don't, and sometimes it's as good as it'll get. Your face is beautiful, and the scar seems to have healed a lot since I last saw it. And, if that's as good as it gets, then maybe it's time for you to find peace with it." She gave him a flat stare, but he just smiled. "You can't scare me off."

"I never understood that either," she admitted, studying him carefully. "Generally I can scare anybody off."

He burst out laughing, opened his arms, and she walked in, feeling a sense of homecoming as they closed around her. He held her close as she buried her face against his chest and just hung on for the ride, as the comfort washed over him and hopefully over them both. When she finally took a step back, she looked up at him, blinking back the tears. He smiled and gently wiped them away. "No tears or you'll get me started too."

She nodded. "Maybe later."

"Definitely later. We've got a lot to process," he declared, firming up his tone. "In the meantime, we have other people here, and I don't know if they are privy to this. Do they know?"

She nodded. "They do. Terk wanted to understand how I was able to trust the information, the connection to you, so I had to tell him about Samuel."

He nodded. "It really does make a difference, right?"

"It really does," she agreed, with a nod. "And it just took me a long time to get out of my stubbornness and to see it for what it was, which, in your case, was a cry for help."

When a knock sounded on the motel room door, she let out a startled exclamation and instinctively stepped up close against him, which he loved.

He put an arm around her, held her close, and said, "It should be Calum."

"Yeah, it should be," she conceded, staring at the door with a horrified look. "That doesn't mean it is."

Royal nodded. "I'll go check it out. You stay here."

He walked over to the door, which was locked, and called out, "Who is it?"

"It's Calum," he said, his tone calm on the other side. "My arms are pretty full, so can you open the damn door?"

With that, Royal opened the door and let him inside. As soon as Calum stepped in and saw the two of them, he nodded. "Good, you are both up. Here's some food, and we should eat. Then we need to get a move on."

CHAPTER 10

JANNA SWALLOWED HARD and stared at Calum. "Where would we go?"

"That is one of the things we still have to figure out." He put the jug of coffee and the bags onto the dining table, and then motioned to them. "First off, you need to eat." And, with that, he turned and headed into the other room to check on Bruce. When Calum stepped back out again, he was frowning.

"How is Bruce?" Janna asked, eyeing him instantly.

"Suffering. We need to get him away from here, and he needs medical attention soon."

"We're in Poland," she noted. "Can't we get it for him here?"

Calum shook his head. "No, we're still too close to the Russian border. If we'd gotten deeper into this country, maybe, but just enough people on both sides are likely to be watching the borders," he explained. "We can't take that chance."

She nodded. "Fine. What are our choices then?"

"Terk has somebody coming over, so we'll see what he has to say." Calum motioned at the food again. "Eat something, and help yourself to the coffee. I will go get Rick up."

At that, Rick called out from the other room, "I'm

awake. I'll be there in a minute." When he stumbled out moments later, he looked as if he was ready to go.

Janna frowned, then asked, "Do you guys always fall out of bed, ready to move?"

"Pretty much, yes," Calum replied. "When we're on a job, we do. Anything less than that requires time we usually don't have." He studied her carefully. "Will it take much to pack you up?"

She snorted. "Pack what? I don't even have a toothbrush."

He smiled. "Nope. And that's good in a way, so we don't leave behind evidence of our passing through here. With any luck, we'll be out of here in a few minutes."

"I thought we would stay for a bit, so these guys could heal," she protested, looking at Royal in concern. "He's a long way from being ready to run again."

"We were, but I don't like anything about this place," Calum shared. "I woke up this morning, feeling that tug on my senses. That signal means we need to move."

"In that case we do need to move," Royal agreed easily. He looked over at her and smiled. "And I'm fine."

She rolled her eyes at that. "You're fine, like I'm fine," she muttered.

"Are you not fine?" Rick asked, stopping to study her. "Because if you've got any problems, you need to tell us right now."

"You mean any *other* problems?" she quipped.

He narrowed his gaze and nodded. "Yeah, any *other* problems. That works."

"I'm fine," she stated.

But Rick wasn't content with that. He read her energy for a long moment, then finally gave her shrug, as if to say,

Whatever. Then he sat down to eat some breakfast wraps. After the men had had two each, and she'd had one, at least six were left.

She looked over at Calum. "Did you mean to buy this much?"

"Yep, I sure did. I probably should have bought more to take with us. I don't know when we'll come across food again."

She winced at that. "Right. It feels as if we've already been shorted a few meals."

He laughed. "But remember that we could be forced out of here in five minutes."

Without warning, the motel room door opened, and a man stepped in, closing the door behind him. She bolted over to where Royal sat. He pulled her closer, as he looked over the stranger, his gaze hard. Yet Rick and Calum appeared to be completely comfortable with the newcomer. They hadn't even moved an inch, and that surprised her.

The man stepped forward and gave her a clipped nod. "I'm Riff."

She frowned at him. "You're part of Terk's team, aren't you?"

"Sometimes," he replied, with half a smile. "And sometimes I'm just a pain in the ass."

At that, Rick stated, "You're always a pain in the ass, but you're *our* pain in the ass."

Riff snorted, then announced, "I've got wheels."

Calum and Rick got up, quickly cleaned up everything that they could, then grabbed a cloth and wiped off the surfaces of everything. Calum nodded at her. "Go get anything that you've got in the other rooms."

She headed to the bedroom and the bathroom, checking

to see if anything was here. She put her dry underwear in her pocket and rejoined the men. "It's clear."

The men brushed past her and checked as well, and, within minutes, they were ready to go.

"What will we do about Bruce?" she asked. "He's in rough shape."

"That's one of the reasons we're moving as fast as we are now. His energy is sinking, and, if we have any hope of keeping that man alive, we need to get him more help."

"Here in Poland?" she asked.

"No," Riff stated. "I've got wheels, but then I've also got wings."

Nonplussed, she stared at him as he walked into the other room, scooped up Bruce as if he weighed absolutely nothing, and stepped to the front door. The other men grabbed the leftover food and were immediately at her side, nudging her out. She took one last look around and followed them down the steps to the vehicle.

She whispered to Calum, "Does Riff really work for you?"

"*With* us," he clarified. "Remember that we operate as a team. We're not so much about bosses."

She laughed. "And yet Terk …"

"Terk's a man unto himself," Calum noted, with half a smile. "He's also a loyal friend and has saved my life more than a few times. So, if Terk says, *Jump*, we don't waste a moment asking, *How high?* We just jump."

"And that has saved you all these years?"

"Absolutely," he stated. "Our instincts are like that. We know who we can trust because we've been together for a long time."

She studied Riff, who even now placed Bruce in the back

seat of a large Suburban. "And you trust him?"

"Yes, I do. Besides," Calum added, as he gave her a grin, "we're out of other options at the moment."

She winced and nodded. "*Great*, that's not exactly how I want to make decisions in life."

"And yet you have, and you do," Calum pointed out. "Instincts let you get close to Royal, so don't discard them now."

ROYAL PUT ALL the personal information Janna had given him in the back of his mind, as they drove carefully through the city that was slowly waking up to a new day. When they came to an airstrip, he almost felt himself relax. But he also knew that this hand-off would likely be one of the most dangerous so far. He got out and walked around to help Janna, but she was already out and looking to help him. He smiled. "I'm fine."

"Right," she muttered. She joined the others headed for the plane and asked, "Who's flying?"

"I am," replied Riff.

She stopped and stared at him.

He gave her a smile. "Yeah, so, if you don't trust me, don't get on."

She snorted at that, looking back at the others. "He's really easy to get along with, isn't he?"

"Nope, he sure isn't," Calum stated, with a smile, while he carried Bruce this time. "But Riff's about all we've got at the moment, so best to play nice."

"*Great*," she muttered. "How is it his résumé hit the hire pile?"

Calum burst out laughing. "Maybe you'll find out firsthand on this ride, but I sure hope not."

She winced at that. "Good point. I probably don't want to see Riff in action, do I?"

"No, you sure don't. However, when we're in trouble, he's the guy we want on our side for sure."

She sighed at that. "Fine, but this isn't easy. He makes Rick seem like the welcome wagon."

"Nothing is easy about this situation," Rick declared. "And it wasn't easy for us to work with you either, by the way. Still, Riff is part of our team, and, if you don't like it, find your own way home, sister." And, with that declaration, he opened the plane door and stepped aside, so Calum could carry Bruce in.

As she stepped into the plane, she looked around, surprised to find that it was quite nice. Her surprise was noted by the others, as she settled into her seat and buckled up, happy that Royal sat down beside her.

He gave her a gentle smile and said, "It's all good."

"Says you," she muttered. "It would be easier if I had some idea what was going on."

When everybody was inside and buckled up, Rick and Calum headed to the front of the plane. She looked over at Royal and asked, "So, they all three sit up there?"

Royal shook his head. "They're probably making plans, or maybe Riff is briefing them."

She winced. "So, we're not on their team, are we?"

"At some point in time, you just have to trust the ones you started out with," Royal stated, shaking his head. "We don't really have a whole lot of choice. As much as I don't know these men, I do know that they are part of Terk's team, and I'm happy to have them with us. So I'm good with that."

"I'm good too," she added. "I just want to get the hell out of here a whole lot faster, rather than be sitting ducks." She shifted in her seat, looking out the window at the airstrip below them. She saw no sign of anybody, but that unease just wouldn't leave her alone.

"Are you feeling insecure about something?" Royal asked her curiously.

"Just everything," she replied. "It's been a long haul to get to this point, and I don't want anything to go wrong in the meantime."

"You and me both," Royal said, with a smile. "Yet we still have a long way to go."

"And we haven't taken to the air yet."

But the words were no sooner out of her mouth, when Rick joined them and sat down beside Bruce, placing a hand on his neck to check that he was okay. The fact that Bruce appeared to be comatose worried her, and yet she wondered if that wasn't the better place for him to be. "I presume your people are keeping him in that state?" she asked Rick.

He nodded. "It's easier for travel purposes."

"Is it good for Bruce though?" she muttered.

"None of this is good for him, but getting him home again is the priority, and that's a whole different story. He needs to remain unconscious for a little bit more."

"What about papers?" she asked. "We don't have anything for him, do we?" At that, she turned and looked at Royal. "What about you?"

He shook his head. "I don't have a passport or ID either," he muttered. "That's just the way life is at the moment."

"Sure." She sighed, sat back, and closed her eyes, focusing on her breathing exercises. When the plane lifted off moments later, she finally felt some of her tension easing back. She opened her eyes and smiled. "Good, I was really afraid we wouldn't make it up."

"Why is that?" Rick asked, looking at her.

She shrugged. "Just that feeling of something going wrong."

His gaze narrowed on her. "It would be much better if you would say things like that *before* we lift off."

Surprised, she frowned. "But I didn't have any reason for it, nothing to back it up. I didn't have any tangible reason to feel that way, and it's not as if you'll listen to me if I just say something *feels* wrong."

"You might be wrong about that. Besides, this is what we do, and our feelings and our instincts are very important."

"I didn't know what to say. I looked around and wondered if we were being followed."

"Did you see anything?" Rick asked.

She shook her head. "No, I didn't."

He seemed to relax a little bit more at that. "If you get any more of those feelings, let me know immediately, okay? *Please.*"

Feeling as if she'd done something wrong, she nodded and whispered, "I'm sorry."

He shrugged. "If somebody is out there, we'll deal with it," he stated, his tone crisp. "But I don't want you to keep us in the dark about what you're feeling ever again. What we need to do is get someplace where Bruce can get care, and we sure don't need anybody delaying us."

She wouldn't argue with that. As she watched the ground disappear below them, she asked, "Where are we heading to, by the way?"

"We're hoping to make it back to England," Rick shared, "but we won't do it in one fell swoop."

"Oh," she whispered. "That's too bad."

"Yep, it sure is. We'll stop in Holland at a private airport and refuel. If all is well, we should make it to England in one trip from there."

She didn't say anything more but nodded.

"You might as well get some sleep," Rick suggested. "I don't know what the rest of the day will bring."

"Fine," she said. With that tidbit of information, she sank back, closed her eyes, and tried to rest, but it was hard. She shifted uneasily several times, and, when she opened her eyes again, Rick stared at her intently. She glared right back at him. "Now what's the matter?"

"*You*. You can't calm down."

"No, I can't. Why is that?"

"In your world, when you say something *feels wrong*, how does that relate to your ability to calm down?"

She blinked several times. "I don't know," she admitted cautiously. "It's not exactly something I'm accustomed to discussing or even recognizing."

"Close your eyes and give it some serious thought," Rick replied. "And this would be a really good time to consider more about your affinity with metal things."

"Oh." She blinked, as she looked around at the plane. The *metal* plane. "It's not something that I ever really did much with, but I can tell when I'm near them and whether it's energy I can use or not."

"Which is also bizarre."

"Yes, you guys told me that earlier," she noted, with a sigh. "Supposedly that energy is way harder to utilize, and it should be much easier for me to use Mother Nature's energy than something metallic or mechanical. I can't tell you anything more than I already have," she stated in exasperation. "I get that you want me to figure out if something is wrong out there. I can tell you that I feel as if absolutely something is wrong, but I don't know what it is. Honestly, it could be at the other end, when we land."

At that, his eyebrows shot up. "If you are picking up something along that line, you definitely need to tell us beforehand."

"If I knew what I was picking up, then I would. So far, it's nothing more than … a case of nerves."

Nodding, Rick didn't say anything for a moment. "Just keep it in mind though, okay?"

Not sure what else she was supposed to do with that information, she nodded and sat back.

Rick added, "We'll be hours in the air, so go ahead and rest."

"I would, except you keep staring at me like that," she muttered, glaring at him.

His lips quirked. "I'm checking out your energy, not so much to see if you're lying, but to see if anything else is going on there."

"Checking out my energy?" she asked, her eyebrows shooting up. "Why don't you check out Bruce's?"

"I already have, and Bruce doesn't have anything to hide."

She stared at him, feeling her heart shrink inside a little bit. "Neither do I. And believe me when I say, I don't trust you any more than you trust me. I don't have any reason to trust anybody in this world," she snapped, glaring at him. "And certainly not arrogant males."

His lips twitched yet again. "Maybe not, but you've come a long way in terms of your friend beside you, so we *arrogant males* can't be all bad."

She flushed at that. "There's still time to see your bad side."

"Maybe so," Rick agreed cheerfully.

He said that almost too cheerfully.

"Yet I'm much more inclined to believe you when I see some temper flaring. You're a little too contained for my liking." And, with that, he settled into his seat again.

She frowned at him. *Too contained?* What the hell did that mean? She was anything but contained. Something was seriously wrong if he thought she looked too complacent, too contained. Still, it was his problem, not hers, and yet she had learned to trust him to some degree.

She had trusted men in her life in many ways and had been badly burned. She had trusted in Royal, and yet that particular trust hadn't been broken. She couldn't blame him for anything that had happened, and what had been created between them had truly been a gift for her, so that her pregnancy on her own was not even an issue. Maybe she didn't have that many trust issues after all. It would just take some time, which was what Royal had pointed out.

Trying to shove it all the way into the back of her brain, she closed her eyes and relaxed, even falling asleep for a bit. She jostled awake at one point, and, looking around, she touched the hull of the plane. She closed her eyes, instinctively sending and receiving calming energy. When she opened them again, Rick was staring at her.

He nudged his chin toward her hand, touching the plane. "Problems?"

She frowned and dropped her hand.

"If there is," he noted, "it would help if we knew."

"I don't have any advanced warnings," she explained tiredly. "I mean, putting my hand on the hull of the plane was just an instinctual move, a natural move, so I'm sorry if I worried you."

"Oh no, feel free to do it," he said. "As long as you're keeping me alive, I'm good." And, with that, he closed his eyes again.

She frowned. "What is your problem with me anyway?"

He opened them and faced her. "*Trust.* An awful lot is going on in your world. A lot of blame, a lot of anger and anguish," he shared. "I can see all that. I can see it churning around through your system."

"I'm sure things are churning around in everyone's system, yours included."

"Sure, but yours are unresolved, and that makes you more unstable than the others. It would have been better if you had dealt with some of that crap before you came on this mission," he explained. "I can see a lot of it is tied to your need to help Royal. Now that you have done that, maybe it'll be easier for me to see what's really behind all this."

She stared at him in astonishment. "Wow, you see all that?"

"Yeah, *all that*," he confirmed. "We all have abilities, and we all see things. And because we're all so very different, our skills and abilities are different as well. Some of us can see things easily. Some of us see things that aren't easy to see at all," he murmured. "Some of us get a flood of information without even trying. Others work very hard to get the tiniest thing. However, as long as my friends and family are working to keep you safe, I want to ensure you're working to keep us safe as well."

"I am," she stated in astonishment. "I can't believe after all this that you would even doubt that."

"But knowing that trust is a big issue for you, I worry about projection. So I'm checking every step of the way to confirm you are who you say you are on the inside." And, with that, he closed his eyes, once again ignoring her.

She let her breath out in a noisy gust, wanting to smack him for his words that were so jarring, yet potentially accurate.

As if on cue he opened his eyes and added, "I wouldn't do that if I were you."

"What? You read minds now too?"

"Yeah, though it doesn't take a mind reader to know you probably very much want to slug me," he shared, with a chuckle, his lips twitching. "I still wouldn't take it kindly." And again he shut his eyes.

She looked over at Royal to see his eyes open and his lips twitching as well. She glared at him. "You too?"

"Not at all," he replied gently, "but he doesn't know you the way I do."

She rolled her eyes at that. "Not sure you know me that well either."

"Maybe, but I'm planning on getting to know you a whole lot more," he teased.

That made her face flush. She squeezed his hand, then slumped in her seat. "It's frustrating being around people who know things about you that you don't want them to know."

"But you already told them, pretty much."

She nodded. "Yes. Not that I necessarily wanted to, but …"

"So, the problem is, you feel vulnerable now because

people know things about you, and you're feeling as if they'll judge you for it, which they won't. So, really the bottom line is that you need to just relax and let life happen. It doesn't always have to be traumatizing, and it need not be a competition either. We're heading toward a fun and happy place, so maybe you should just relax and let it be."

"Maybe when we get you back to normal," she conceded, looking at him. "Yet every time I see you and Bruce, I see just what a shitty world we live in."

"That may be, but every time I look at you and Bruce and Calum and Rick and Riff," Royal pointed out, "I realize just how many good things are in this life. For every negative, for every bad thing that happens, I can always find something good to focus on instead."

She sighed. "Right? I just need to do that, don't I?"

"For that to happen," he said, "you'll probably need to let go of the guilt and the grief. Honestly, I'm not sure we ever let go of grief. … I think that you'll probably always carry it with you, but you'll do it in such a way that we'll honor that small life that was in our world for too short a time. We must learn to live with all of it though, the good, the bad, and the ugly."

The fact that he was using the word *we* made the tears come to her eyes, as she stared out of the plane. "The guilt," she began, "is crippling. Only so much I can do with that, and yet it's never enough. You wake up one morning, and it's all over," she whispered, her voice breaking again. "And once again you try to do everything you can, but you feel helpless, useless, as if absolutely nothing and nobody is out there for you. So, whatever. If they judge me for it, they judge me for it."

Eyes still closed, Rick replied, "Nobody's judging you

for anything. My only concern is whether you're a danger to us or those around us on this trip." He sat up and faced her. "Don't read more into my assessment than you need to. I'm just doing my job."

She almost laughed at that but realized he was serious. She nodded. "Thanks for that."

"Nobody has the right to judge you for anything," Rick explained. "Don't let them. You've been hurt multiple times, but you do have the option of letting that go at any point in time, choosing to live in the present and into the future. You did that when you came to us to help Royal. Don't waste this second opportunity." With that, he closed his eyes again and sank back into whatever stupor he'd come from.

She was still staring at him, trying to figure out how that would work, when Royal squeezed her fingers and said, "He's right, you know?"

"I know he is," she agreed. "I just didn't want to deal with it." Then she gave him a cheeky grin. "However, it is very true that I don't want to ruin this second chance with you."

"Good," Royal declared. "I wasn't planning on giving you the option anyway."

Startled, she asked him, "Really?"

"I told you that we needed to spend some time together, and I meant it." He raised his hand, as if taking an oath. "Believe me that I mean it. I'll also talk to Terk about working with him after this."

At that, Rick opened his eyes. "He'll probably be quite happy to take you on, and we do need more men on the team," he noted, "though you're a long way away from healed up and ready to work."

"Got it." Royal nodded. "I'll heal up, and probably pretty fast, I would think."

"With or without help?" Rick asked, a note of humor in his tone. "We've become accustomed to that healing assistance, but I'm not sure you have."

"No, I haven't, but I'm more than happy to join in on that train. To know that amount of healing is available out there"—he shook his head—"that's huge."

Hearing his words, Janna realized just how much they owed Terk and his team, even Rick, who had seemed so incredibly unfriendly to her. Yet she wasn't sure it was about her as much as the circumstances, which he had explained. She gently rubbed the metal surface of the plane's hull, not even realizing what she was doing, until both men studied her again. She flushed and dropped her hand.

"By all means," Rick said, "if you want to connect to it, do it. I've just never seen anybody connect to metal."

"No, and neither have I. I really … never had a chance to exercise my gift," she shared. "The only time I've ever really utilized it was when I was in a car accident."

"What happened?" Rick asked.

She shrugged. "Let's just say the accident didn't happen."

At that, they both blinked, and Rick sat straight up. "You do realize that you'll need to provide more of an explanation than that."

"Do I?" she asked, shaking her head. "Maybe later."

"Or not," Rick countered. "If you could potentially stop this plane from crashing, all of us want to know about that."

She winced. "How the hell would I do that?" she asked in horror. "Even if I did, it would mean that I'd had prior practice in order to know how to do that, and I've never had a plane incident."

"Yet you had a car incident …"

She shrugged. "But no accident occurred. When I told it to move out of the way of oncoming vehicles that were getting in a big pile up, somehow I ended up on the other side of a fence."

They just stared at her.

She shrugged. "The thing is, I wasn't in the driver's seat, so I'm not sure what I could do. I just know that, back then, I could do something, and I did it, but I don't know what or how. Now I'm sitting here, wondering if I should be doing something because my hand keeps wanting to touch this damn bird we're flying in," she shared, "and I don't know what the problem is."

"If there's a problem, let us know ahead of time, please," Rick repeated. "I'm really not up for a crash landing."

She stared at him and winced. "Yeah, neither am I."

"Good." Rick nodded. "In that case I'm going back to sleep."

"How can you possibly sleep?" she asked, staring at him. "You open your eyes every five minutes."

"You've heard that phrase about sleeping with one eye open? Well, it's the same idea," he stated, with a smirk. "Don't let it bother you. I'll take whatever time I get, especially when you're keeping an eye on everything else going on."

"*Sure*," she muttered. "You say that, but …" She let her words drift off with a shrug.

Rick studied her for a moment and then closed his eyes and headed back into whatever dreamland state he was accustomed to going into.

She looked over at Royal to see him fading off as well. Dumbfounded, she shook her head. "Wow, is it just me?"

"Nope, not just you," Calum called out from the cabin, as he slowly walked toward her.

She frowned. "Shouldn't you be flying the plane?"

"Nope, not me. Riff has it all handled for now, and I just wanted to check in and see how you guys were getting on."

"Rick's sleeping with his eyes open, so I don't know how that works," she muttered. "The other two have been drifting in and out."

"I'm here," Royal said, his eyes closed. "Just trying to get as much rest as possible."

Rick joined in and said, "Calum, since you're with us now, you need to have a serious talk with her about metal energy. She keeps touching the bird."

She glared at Rick. "See? He never really sleeps at all. And, Jesus, Rick, did you have to make it sound so weird and wrong?"

He opened his eyes and replied with a distinct note of amusement in his tone, "I wasn't even going to bring that aspect of it up, but, hey, if you want to go in that direction, we certainly could."

She snorted and looked over at Calum. "Your friend here has a problem, well, a number of problems, which I'm sure you already know about, since it's painfully evident to me, and I barely even know him."

Calum smiled gently. "A lot of people would suggest that everybody has a number of problems, and I would agree that all of us do—including you, I might add."

She sighed. "Yes. Finally someone had the courage to just say it out loud. It's about time. Thank you."

Chuckling, Calum looked around at the others, then shook his head. "Okay, so back to the point brought up by my helpful but not always tactful colleague. So, why do you keep touching the metal?"

"I don't even know," she cried out. "I told you before I seem to have an affinity for metals."

"Right."

"I can't really explain it and have nothing to back this up, but honestly, I am a little worried," she shared, feeling embarrassed and frustrated, knowing her thoughts wouldn't likely go over well.

"She thinks the plane will crash," Rick chimed in, eyes closed, clearly enjoying the moment.

At that, Calum looked at her wide-eyed, and she shrugged. "Damn it, Rick. Why do you have to be such a jerk when it comes to me? Why don't you go to sleep for a few minutes, so the adults in the room can have a conversation?" Turning her attention back to Calum, she took a deep breath. "It's not that I think it'll crash," she explained, "but I keep touching it and trying to …" She groaned. "Now here is where you'll really think I'm nuts."

"Try me."

"It's just …" She sighed. "When I put my hand on the hull, I'm just telling it that everything's okay, that it can just keep functioning as it is, and that nothing bad will happen to it."

"You're giving the plane life?" Calum asked.

She opened her eyes wider. "It's energy, I guess," she replied in confusion. "All energy is life, right?" At that, she couldn't help but return the stares coming her way from both Rick and Calum, as they studied her. "Am I wrong?" she asked. "I mean, it just seemed like that was the truth."

"The truth is, in many cases, a different perception for other people," Calum replied. "If that's the truth for you, then we're happy to go with it."

She snorted. "Now it sounds as if you're just placating me."

He grinned. "No, I'm not, but, while we're in the air, and there could be a problem with this bird, you just keep touching it and telling it that all is good," Calum instructed, a grin on his face and a smile in his tone. "Not a one of us will argue or will put up a fight if we land safely. Then again, if we don't"—he turned to face her—"a few people might be asking if there was more you could have done."

She glared at him. "That's not fair either."

"Nothing's fair in life, not at all," Calum stated, with that cheerfulness again. "But, if you can do something to help us land safely, please do." And, with that, he headed up to the cabin again to check in with Riff.

She looked over, but Rick had his eyes closed, and so did Royal. Looking around, she realized that they were right. Of all the things that any of them could be doing right now, getting some rest was probably the best choice. Besides keeping an eye on the plane—however that worked—sleep was definitely the best thing for her. With that decided, she was more than happy to crash herself.

ROYAL WOKE YET again in the plane, shifting in his seat as he worked to get the kinks out of his back. He was tired and sore, and the trip was taking way longer than his body could handle. If he could lie down, it would help a lot. Food, coffee, anything at all would help a lot too, but everybody else was in a light slumber. Royal got up and used the bathroom, then slowly made his way back to his seat.

As he sat down, Calum poked his head around from the cabin of the airplane. “Are you doing okay?”

Royal nodded. “Yeah, I’ll make it. Any idea how much longer we’ll be in the air?”

“We’ll be touching down here pretty quick, but only to fuel up. Then we’ll be up in the air again and on our way home.”

Royal nodded. “Thank you, … for all you guys have done.”

Calum nodded and didn’t say anything beyond that.

For Royal, this had been a strange introduction to Terk and his team, but, hey, Royal and Bruce were both alive, and that was way the hell more than Royal had expected.

When the light came on to put on their seatbelts, he heard Riff’s voice come over the intercom.

“Heads up, guys. We’ll be starting our descent soon and should be on the ground in about twenty minutes,” he announced. “So, everybody buckle in, and hopefully this will be a smooth glide down.”

As soon as they got closer to the runway, Royal gently nudged Janna. She opened her eyes and blinked at him owlishly. He smiled, completely overwhelmed with love as he looked at this woman he had walked away from and had regretted it ever since. “Hey, just a warning that we’ll be landing.”

Quickly she scrambled to orient herself, shifting to look out the window and smiling in delight. “Now that,” she said, looking pleased, “is a really nice thing to hear. I was afraid this trip would be very long.”

“It was,” Royal declared, with a laugh, “but you slept pretty well.”

“Did I?” She checked around and shrugged. “I don’t

even know what time it is."

"It's two in the afternoon," Rick replied, from across the aisle. "And great news. So far, the plane has held."

She flushed at his teasing comment but instinctively touched the hull, then smiled.

"How is it?" Rick asked.

"How's what?" she challenged.

"The plane, is it happy?" Rick asked.

She shrugged. "It's not unhappy, at least at the moment."

"Good to know," Rick replied. "We won't be down for long, but you'll at least get to walk around a bit to loosen up your legs, and then we're taking off again."

"The sooner, the better, as far as I'm concerned," she said. "Will the government have paperwork ready for us when we hit England?"

"That's the hope, though it doesn't mean things will go quite so smoothly as that," Rick noted. "However, once we've landed, they'll have a hard time kicking us back out again."

"Most of us shouldn't be too hard to sort out," Janna said, "but I don't know about Bruce."

"Bruce is in rough shape. If nothing else, he should be granted emergency asylum from persecution," Rick stated.

Janna snorted. "Yet you and I both know it's not nearly as simple as that, not when dealing with governments."

"No, it sure isn't," Rick agreed, "but we have people working on it."

"Is Terk helping?" Janna asked.

"Of course. I get that you probably don't really understand the scope of what we do," Rick suggested, "but we always come from the heart and try our best to do what is right. That is precisely why we have our own company now, so we aren't forced to deal with governments and their versions of navigating between right and wrong."

She smiled at that. "I'm not sure governments have the ability or even the desire to do that credibly," she stated. "The nature of the beast is something very different from that, and their goals and objectives are too often influenced by power and politics."

"I can't disagree with that assessment, but we're working hard to change the perception of the industry," Rick shared. "You could always come aboard and help us, you know?"

"What would I do?" she asked. "I don't have anywhere near the skills you guys do. I'm not even in the same league."

"I'm not so sure." Rick laughed. "I've never seen anybody reassure a plane before, certainly not to check that it was happy."

She frowned, unsure whether he was joking or not, and then shrugged because it didn't matter. She had told him how she had worked with vehicles and had certainly found cars for them when they needed them. So this plane was just another aspect. A few minutes later, when the plane touched down, she got up and stretched, then walked out onto the tarmac as everybody exited, leaving Bruce on board while they quickly fueled up.

There was some paperwork to be dealt with, which Calum and Rick took off to take care of, even as Riff walked around the tarmac, talking on the phone, frowning the whole time. When he came over to her, she couldn't help but ask, "Problems?"

He shrugged. "I hope not. You tell me." He looked at her quizzically for a moment. "Interesting energy."

She stared at him. "What does that mean?"

He shrugged. "Dunno. I've never seen anything like yours before."

"Are you talking about my energy or my face?"

"Nope, seen the face before," he stated. "I was shown a picture so I could find you. It's not nearly as bad as you're afraid it is." Riff's phone rang again, and he answered it, stepping away for some privacy.

"So you say," she muttered, wondering if it was true and worrying that she might need other people to make that assessment for her. With a groan, she was likely on the verge of losing it on several fronts. So, she walked closer to where Royal was standing and stretching. She came up behind him. "How are you feeling?"

"I've been better," he said, turning to her and opening his arms. She stepped in, and he just held her close.

"I don't know why," she murmured, "but it feels like a homecoming every time you do that."

"That's because we belong together," he declared. "It just took some foolishness to make us realize it. I'm so glad that it did."

"I realized it before," she muttered, "but I was too damn stupid to do anything about it."

He tapped her lips. "Enough of that."

She nodded. "You're right. It absolutely is enough, and I promise I'm working on it."

He stared at her silently.

She shrugged. "Everybody keeps telling me that my face doesn't matter, so I think it's time to let some things go. Like when I told you that Sam's presence made a huge difference? … It really did, but I don't think I updated my history in the way that I should have."

"Hey, that's something all of us need to do. Don't take it

personally. After all, we are all humans and bound to make mistakes from time to time."

She smiled. "I want to ensure I don't repeat those same mistakes."

"I'm all for that," he agreed, with a smile. He pointed at Calum and Rick, walking toward them. "Now we'll head back up in the plane and hopefully get to England just fine."

When two black vehicles entered the airport at a high speed, she looked over and groaned. "Now we've got trouble."

Royal called over to Riff. Frowning, he got off the phone and walked closer.

"Anybody know who they are?" Riff asked everyone, as they joined together.

"Nope, I don't," she said, as she edged toward the plane. "However, we need to leave."

"We never got Bruce off, so you head on up and get in," Riff suggested. "We'll handle this."

"Yeah, just as long as *handling this* means you guys getting us all the hell out of there. Like now."

Riff eyed her. "You feel trouble?"

"Yeah," she said, "but I'm not exactly impartial."

"Get back on board," Riff ordered, as he waited for the vehicles to get closer.

Janna and Royal both got in, leaving Rick, Calum, and Riff on the tarmac. She watched as several arguments ensued outside, and she was afraid it had to do with paperwork, which would be more of a problem than anybody realized. When a series of phone calls were made, she looked at Royal. "It's not looking good."

Royal nodded. "I have a few skills that might help, but I'm pretty weak."

"I don't know what you can do in a case like this," she said, looking at him. "Yet, if you have any tricks up your sleeve, it would probably be a good time to try them."

He looked at her and asked, "You got energy to spare?"

"For you, always," she said and held out her hand.

He took it and walked them to the open door of the plane. Nobody out there on the tarmac seemed to even notice that Royal and Janna were here. When he squeezed her hand, she watched energy zing out toward the two new arrivals. Surprised, she watched as their demeanor completely changed. All of a sudden, calls ended, and phones were put away, then laughter came. Waving their hands, the men suddenly got back into their vehicles and started to back up.

Royal whispered, "I can't hang on to this much longer. Can you get the others back inside the plane?"

She called to the men urgently, and they boarded the plane. "Guys, we need to get out of here fast. Royal did something to change their minds or to change something anyway," she explained, "but he's all in and about to collapse."

Just as she said that, Royal dropped, caught by Calum on the way down, breaking Royal's link with Janna. Riff and Rick bolted to the cabin of the plane, started the engine, and they took off.

CHAPTER 11

As they landed in England, Calum shouted from the cabin, "Heads up."

Janna watched as an official-looking vehicle drove toward them on the tarmac. "*Great.* Does this mean we'll be separated?"

Calum nodded. "Probably, bound to be a debriefing, if nothing else."

She stared at him in shock. "I didn't think far enough ahead," she cried out. "This shouldn't be allowed."

Calum eyed her silently.

Royal took Janna's hand. "If they're paying money to save my ass, you can bet they'll want intel as to what happened."

She frowned at that. "But you're still injured, so sick and terribly weak."

"They do have medical facilities."

She shook her head. "Yeah, but that kind of medical is not a good thing for you, not as an energy worker."

He stared at her. "Okay. So now you are freaking me out. What's going on?"

"I don't know," she admitted, feeling like throwing a temper fit. She looked around the plane that she had mentally kept connected to the whole time, more so because of her own fears that somebody would be an asshole and would do something, rather than any actual possibility. Yet, as she sat here, not wanting to cause anybody any undue stress, she just basically kept a hand on the plane the whole way to England. She knew that they didn't really understand what that was all about, but it was hard for her *not* to keep that physical connection. It was just the right thing to do. It felt just as right to do that as it felt completely wrong to let Royal leave in the vehicles coming toward them.

She quickly stepped forward, as the plane slowly rolled up toward the vehicles. She looked over at Rick and declared, "They can't take Royal."

He studied her mildly. "If you've got a reason to stop it, I want to hear it."

She frowned. "I don't know. It's just wrong."

"And that's your emotions talking," Calum noted, exiting the cockpit. "I'm afraid the government will need a whole lot more than that."

She glared at him. "They shouldn't," she snapped. "Something about this is wrong."

The door opened, and she walked out first. There on the tarmac, several men came closer to talk. The first one, wearing a suit and an overcoat, stared at her. "Good God, who the hell are you?"

"Good God, who the hell are you?" she snapped right back.

His eyebrows soared, as he looked behind her at the rest of the team coming out of the plane.

Calum smiled at the newcomer. "Hey, Jonas. I presume you're here because of the CIA."

"Yeah, although I'm not sure I want to be," he admitted, looking back at Janna. "Apparently not everyone is happy to see me."

She shrugged. "Anybody who's trying to take these two men away will get the same attitude." She crossed her arms, as she stood beside Royal. "Why does the CIA want him?"

"For one thing, they negotiated for his release," Jonas replied, looking at her strangely. "I would think you would be happy about that."

"Since I'm the one who initiated this rescue," she snapped, "I can't say I'm particularly happy about the fact that you guys want to take him away."

"He needs to debrief," Jonas stated. "And this is a government issue, not something that you'll be able to stop."

She took a step forward, definitely not a fan of this Jonas, and wasn't surprised when he took a half step back, before asking the men with Janna, "What's going on here?"

"Let's just say that she's invested a lot in making sure that Royal got out of Russia and wants to know for sure that he'll be okay."

"Is there any reason why he wouldn't be okay?" Jonas asked.

"Royal was kidnapped, tortured, and starved," she snapped. "The government didn't seem to give a damn, so why the interest now?"

"I'm with MI6, so it wasn't *our* government," he noted calmly, seeming to understand that some of her emotions were more about the relationship she and Royal had than anything else. "So, you can back off a little bit on that," he declared. "The bottom line is, my hands are tied. No matter what, he's going with us." He turned and looked at Royal. "Are you ready?"

"Depends on where I'm going," he replied easily, "but yes."

At that, Jonas nodded. "You'll be coming with us to

London, where we'll debrief you. I know the CIA has somebody on the way over, now that we've confirmed you're here. We'll pick him up at the airport tomorrow morning."

"Good enough," Royal said.

As he stepped toward the waiting vehicle, Janna stepped up and accompanied him. No way he was going without her.

"Oh, no, no. No you don't," Jonas said, pointing at her. "You weren't part of this deal."

She gave him the sweetest of smiles. "It'll take a better man than you to stop me."

He stopped, his jaw almost literally dropping. "You did hear me say this is a government matter, right?" He was troubled and very frustrated. "Please understand that I can even order you to jail for interfering or disregarding instructions."

"And again," Janna repeated, "it'll take a better man than you and anybody you brought along to make that happen. I'm staying with Royal. He's been to hell and back, and nobody will do that to him again."

Jonas let out a breath, as he raised a hand, pushing his hair off his forehead. "I wasn't expecting to have you along."

Janna declared, "Being part of the government means being adaptable, so this is a really good time to adapt."

Calum and Rick both laughed. "She does have a point, and she has gone through a lot to ensure Royal got back, safe and sound. But she also doesn't like *any* governments very much, so this is potentially a problem."

"But it's not *my* government involved in this," Jonas said, frowning at her. "Besides, I'm not sure I even have clearance to take you along."

"In that case, let's all head to Terk's," Janna suggested.

"Whoa, whoa, whoa, no you're not," Jonas declared.

"I'm under orders too."

Turning to him, she asked, "You got a problem with Terk?"

There was a stillness, while everybody waited for the answer. Jonas glared at her and then shook his head in resignation. "Oh no, that's not fair. Of course I have no problem with Terk, but this is not my deal."

"No? So, if it's not your deal, we don't need to listen to you then, do we?"

Jonas raised his hands in frustration. "God. Why are women always so difficult?"

She snorted. "Not all women are difficult and certainly not all the time," she snapped. "Right about now I'm quite happy to be an exception."

He glared at her. "I'll make some phone calls."

"You do that," she said, standing her ground. With a smile, she turned to Royal and put an arm around his shoulders, as he tucked her up close and kissed her gently.

"It's okay. I'll find you when I'm released."

"No. Something is wrong here. I know it."

At that, Rick and Calum stepped closer. "Look, Janna. We deal with Jonas all the time," Calum explained, "so, if you've got any inkling of something wrong here, we need to know what it is."

"Definitely something is wrong," she snapped. "I just don't know how or when it will play out. I can't leave Royal."

"Details on what is wrong would definitely help," Rick pointed out. "Nebulous doesn't really do it for us."

"No, it doesn't do it for me either," she snapped, glaring at him. "But I can tell you that something is wrong and that will have to do for now."

When Jonas came back, he said, "I'm not sure what's going on, but they seem to be okay to allow you to come with us."

"Good," Janna replied, inclining her head. "Smart choice."

He glared at her. "Look. I don't need any trouble."

"I'm not planning on giving you any trouble, as long as you let me stay with Royal," she explained. "My only interest is looking out for Royal. He's been through enough already."

"And yet I'll remind you again that it wasn't us," Jonas replied, studying her closely, as if trying to figure out what made her tick. He looked over at Calum and asked, "Is there anything I should know about her?"

They all just grinned and shrugged.

"Does she work for Terk?" Jonas asked, suddenly suspicious, eyeing her as if she might blow up, like a time bomb or something.

She gave him the sweetest smile ever, although it made her look a bit menacing. "I'm considering it."

He almost instantly backed up and glared at the others. "You know how I feel about all this woo-woo stuff," he muttered. "Why is there another one?"

"We always find another one," Janna declared, "particularly when everything went so wrong for Royal."

He nodded. "Fine, you can stand guard. That will save me some man-hours." He turned and looked at the other men. "What about you guys? Are you coming or are you off to see Terk?"

Rick studied him. "I'm coming along."

She turned and looked at Calum and Riff. The other two nodded. "We're coming too."

Jonas stopped, then frowned. "Okay, that's weird. What

are you guys not telling me? What is it I need to know?"

"Something is wrong here," Riff declared, stepping forward. "We're not sure what the deal is, but we won't just let it go, not without a little oversight."

Jonas stared at them in astonishment. "You guys know me. We've worked together a lot, and I know there isn't anything wrong. So what the hell is this?"

"When we say, *Something is wrong*, we mean, *she* can sense it, and that means, *something is wrong*," Riff explained, stepping closer and studying the men still sitting in the vehicle behind him. "How well do you know those guys?"

Jonas didn't look behind him, but his breath leapt out in hard *woosh*. "I don't, but one is a Russian ambassador. He wanted to see you, Royal, and the other is the US liaison," Jonas shared, trying to keep calm. "As I mentioned earlier, the CIA has someone on the way over as well."

At the mention of the Russian ambassador, everybody turned and glared at the vehicle.

Jonas nodded. "I know. He's not who you want to see here. I get it, but we have agreements between countries, and, like everybody else, I have a boss. So I pretty well do what I'm told."

"That may be," Riff replied, "but Janna's right. Something is wrong here."

"You can't honestly think the Russian will do something when we're right here, when he's here in England, do you?"

"Oh, absolutely," Janna declared. "He's planning it right now. I'm just not sure how far he'll go, and what it is that he's hoping to stop from happening."

"Shit," Jonas muttered, looking around. "If it was anybody else telling me this crap, I would have laughed off the whole thing and put my foot down. But, because you're all associated with Terk's team, now you've got my nerves on edge."

"And they should be," she confirmed, stepping closer and looking at the vehicle out of the corner of her eye. "All I can tell you is that something is wrong with that vehicle."

Jonas sighed, shaking his head. "If you guys could ever come up with something more than, *Hey, all I can tell you is something's wrong,*" he began, mimicking Janna's voice, "it would make it a lot easier to explain to people when I need help."

For the first time, she realized just what he was up against, and she smiled. "That's a very good point. We'll ride in that vehicle with them."

"Why is that?" Jonas asked. "Probably not quite enough room for everybody." He was on the verge of losing his cool. "I wasn't expecting everybody to come along."

Janna shrugged. "Neither are they, but somebody's making a rapid change of plans right now." She studied the men, still in the vehicle parked in front of them. She looked back at Rick, Riff, and Calum. "What do you think?"

"Absolutely. We'll all come along." He looked at her and nodded. "That SUV will probably hold all of us."

She looked back at the Suburban. "Great. Three, six, seven, eight, nine, counting Jonas. That's all of us in with the Russian, driven by the US liaison. Good then, we're going as a single unit."

"You sure about this?" Rick asked, eyeing her carefully.

She nodded. "Yeah, that's why I'm going." With that, she led the way to the vehicle.

Behind her, she heard Jonas and the others arguing, as Jonas was looking for some explanation.

She turned to Jonas and added, "Don't mention anything about this to anybody else, do you hear me?" He stopped and glared at her. "I'm serious. The repercussions will be fatal." And, with that, she took Royal's hand and headed over to the Suburban, opened up the big slider door, and they crawled into the back seat. She watched as Riff came out of the plane with Bruce in his arms, then turned her gaze on the two men in the front seat, as the passenger studiously didn't make a sound, and the driver audibly gasped.

"There's another one?" he whispered.

She leaned forward. "Yes, your lovely Russian friends tortured that one too," she said, with a hard look at the passenger.

The Russian turned to look at her. "How did you get involved in this?"

She shrugged. "That may be beyond your pay grade."

The look of astonishment on his face had her smiling as she sat back, but the Russian guy just snorted, as if he wouldn't listen to anything she had to say.

That was the kind of attitude she expected from him anyway. She nodded. "Yeah, you don't like hearing that, do you? That's okay. Not a whole lot I like about seeing you here either."

The other men clambered in around her, and, as they drove off the small airstrip, she checked on Bruce, who even now was unconscious. Worried, she looked back at Riff. "Maybe we should take him to the hospital first."

"That's not happening," Jonas stated. "We have specialists waiting for him."

"How did you know you would need them?"

"Terk told me."

Satisfied with that response, she nodded and settled

back. But there was nothing, absolutely nothing about this scenario that she was comfortable with.

ROYAL WASN'T SURE what had Janna so worried, but since she was defending him, he let it go. Also he could sense the weird energy crawling through the vehicle, so he was totally okay with her preemptive actions. He just wished he'd had the opportunity to ask her more about what was going on, but her gaze remained focused and watchful. The others were on high alert as well. The thought that they were all in the same vehicle worried him, but then he realized that, if the Russian tried anything, that wouldn't go so well for him, since he was with all of them and would get the backlash of whatever happened anyway.

As they drove along, Royal watched, worried as she stretched out a hand toward the front seat, instead of stroking the vehicle. He'd never seen anybody do anything like that. Now she was whispering something to herself too. And the farther they traveled away from the airfield, he felt the tension coil tighter and tighter around them. Something was definitely wrong; he just didn't know what or how to fix it.

He sent out as much calming thoughts as he could, but, with her utilizing her energy on whatever was going on with this vehicle, he was hamstrung as to what he could do to ease the tension. Though maybe it wasn't his job to do anything. He was tired, worn out, frustrated, and just wanted to be alone with her. But he also knew that he was bound by law to do a debriefing. Although, what that debriefing would give MI6, he didn't know because he didn't have any knowledge. The Russians had fought so hard to keep him there, and that distorted Royal's importance. The Russians in the first prison had tortured him for intel he didn't have, and now he would be debriefed again for information. Once again something else he didn't have.

At least he wouldn't be tortured this time. At that thought, he almost winced because there really wasn't any guarantee of that. He could only hope that reason and good sense would rule the day, but he wasn't in a position to feel confident of anything.

When the vehicle slowed at a turnoff, two vehicles came out of nowhere and halted their vehicle. The passengers in each car exited and drew their guns. Jonas swore. But, as Royal looked over at Janna, she was focused on something else.

He whispered, "What's going on?"

"This is an attempt to take something back here, and I think it's you."

"I'm not going anywhere."

At that, the Russian turned, pulling out a handgun, which he pointed at Royal. "You don't have to go back. All we care about is silencing you."

With that, he went to pull the trigger. The vehicle was crammed full of so many bodies, which shifted to get between the gunman and Royal. The Russian hesitated because he couldn't get a clear shot.

Calum grabbed his gun hand. "What the hell do you think you're doing?" he asked. "We went to a lot of trouble to bring this man back from your nightmarish little hellhole, so we sure as hell won't let you just pop him right now."

"It would be a whole lot easier," the Russian stated, glaring at him. "Do you think we will tolerate this? You broke this man out of our prison, someone arrested for treason. That is an unforgivable sin."

"Treason? Really?" Royal asked. "What did I do? Nothing, that's what I did. How about the fact that I was tortured? How about the fact that I was arrested and given no trial or even a lawyer or anybody to help me out? What about the fact that you basically threw away the key and forgot about me? I didn't do anything wrong, and all you guys could do was torture me, trying to get me to say that I did something wrong."

"You're a liar," the Russian said, with a shrug. "In my country, we don't accept liars. Even our law says we could have shot you."

"And yet you didn't, so what was it that you wanted from me that kept me alive all that time? Because, honest to God, I don't know. I don't understand. This had nothing to do with me in the first place. This was all about leverage and government games."

The Russian laughed. "Maybe, but I'm not privy to that either. I just follow orders, the same as everybody else."

The vehicle's side doors were opened as the two gunmen stepped closer and ordered them all out of the vehicle.

She shrugged, then reached out a hand and mentally sent orders to the metal. She didn't know if it would work and had never really planned on it, not until this point in time. But instead of the Russian gunman, she focused on the two drivers, still in the other two vehicles, and that's where she sent her energy. Both vehicles jumped forward, slamming into the two gunmen, now pinned against the SUV. The two were killed instantly.

Calum disarmed the Russian, while Rick and Riff restrained the Russian and the supposed US liaison. Janna looked over at Jonas and gave him a smirk. "See why I needed to come along?" She smiled as beads of sweat appeared on his forehead, but her concern was for Bruce, who opened his eyes slowly and looked at her. She smiled at him. "Hey. Believe it or not, you're in England."

He gave her a brief smile. "Don't tell me. You must be Janna."

She stared at him in shock. "How do you know my name?"

"Ah, that was entirely due to Royal," he murmured. "All he ever talked about was you. Figured that, if he ever got free, he would find you and would make up for lost time. So, if I'm in England, and a beautiful angel is leaning over me, then you must be Royal's angel, and that makes you Janna."

And, with that, Bruce closed his eyes and drifted back into unconsciousness again.

ROYAL STUDIED THE silent crowd, as they waited outside the SUV, as more official cars pulled up. Most of the group, his team, and particularly Jonas and the American attaché, didn't say a word. Everybody kept looking at Janna sideways. Royal didn't.

He stood protectively at her side, hating to admit that he was still so weak, but no way he would leave her to stand alone at this point. He recognized that Calum and Rick were holding strategic positions too, as they all waited for additional teams to come sort out this mess. Not to mention first responders had been called, so ambulances and the coroner were coming to take away the deceased and the injured. The Russian ambassador had nothing good to say and was spouting threats at every question. Janna ignored everyone and stood beside Royal, staring off into space, as if in a fugue state.

Royal wasn't entirely sure that she wasn't in an altered state. He caught several looks from Rick, who was frowning at him, but Royal could do nothing but shrug. As far as he knew, Janna was fine, and this was just her way of buying time and avoiding the advent of whatever was coming next—which Royal could only hope wouldn't be ugly for her, but he didn't know. Then, as he thought about what had just happened, he wasn't sure how anybody could blame her, short of having a significant understanding of energy work. Hell, he didn't think any of them understood her gift.

When yet another vehicle approached, Royal felt the surge of energy as a tall man got out, two others accompanying him, immediately walking toward the group.

Jonas, a look a relief on his face, walked over and muttered, "I'm surprised to see you here, but I'm damn glad." His words were just barely loud enough for Royal to hear.

Royal checked out Janna again, but she was still off in whatever zone she was in. He watched as the men around him, Calum and Rick and Riff, walked over and greeted the tall authoritative man. At that moment, Royal realized this had to be Terk. It was a reasonable assumption, since they'd landed in England, so of course Terk would be here. Honestly, Terk was probably the best person to appear at this particular moment. Somebody needed to explain what the hell was going on in some logical manner because Royal knew that any logical thinking had to be in short supply.

When Terk detached himself from Jonas, Terk and the two men with him all headed toward Janna, Rick, Calum, Riff, and Royal. Terk stopped for a moment, assessed Royal's condition, and gave a slight nod. "Hell of an appearance," he murmured.

Royal gave him a lopsided grin. "Yeah, you're not kidding," he muttered. "Thanks for the rescue."

Terk just nodded and then squatted beside Janna, who now sat on the street, staring off into the distance. He lifted a hand and waved it through her field of vision.

She narrowed her eyes, shifted, and looked over at him. "Yeah, what do you want?" she grumbled.

He gave her a gentle smile, as he whispered, "You know I'm not mad at you, right?"

Her gaze narrowed, as he held her hand. "You have no reason to be mad at me," she muttered. "Besides, what else was I supposed to do?"

The other four men squatted, so this ring of six energy workers were gathered together. Terk's two additional men stood nearby. Janna's gaze went from Rick to Calum to Riff to Terk, then to the two additional men near Terk.

She nodded. "All of you are the same, aren't you?" she asked.

Terk nodded. "They're all members of my team, all my friends and brothers-in-arms," he confirmed. "And very much like you and Royal." Everybody could see the visible hunch of her shoulders, as she pulled them in against his words. He nodded. "And you still have a way to go to accept that."

"Not so much," she muttered finally. "Some of it is an instinctive reaction. Some of it's outright denial, and some is just waiting for the other shoe to drop over this mess."

Terk looked back at Rick. "You want to tell me what happened?"

Rick flashed a grin, looking around to see if anybody else

was close by. Once he was assured that no one was within listening distance, he began, "The official version is that the brakes failed on the two intercepting vehicles, and they jumped forward. The only other version is that the men were hired to take out certain people on this job and decided to throw in the towel at the last minute. So, we can pick and choose one of those." Rick grinned. "The unofficial version," he stated, his gaze turning to Janna, his tone almost too excited, "is that Janna here caused both vehicles to jump forward simultaneously to take out the armed attackers. It was one hell of a trick. I've never seen it happen, and I really wish she would come back to headquarters with us and teach everyone."

At that, she stared at him. "Seriously?"

"Yes," Rick stated. "We have never had anybody with a connection … to speak to mechanical equipment, and it would be incredibly valuable."

She frowned at him. "Are you kidding? While it seemed necessary at the time, it's not something I'm very proud of," she muttered. "Why would I even want to bring it into the light?"

"Because, if you were there with us," Terk said calmly, "you could learn to control it and could do only good with it."

She frowned at the crime scene around her and behind them. "How is this doing good?" she muttered. "Killing people?" She stared up at Royal, her gaze huge, and it broke Royal's heart.

He squeezed her hand gently and replied, "And yet what do you think they would have done to us, had you not stopped them?"

She nodded at him. "That's the only reason I did it. I

really wasn't even sure it would work or that I could even do it," she muttered, still in denial, then shook her head. It seemed to take her a minute to collect her thoughts, and then she looked up, glaring at Terk. "And I know you'll say I could come and join your merry band of crazy men and learn to control it and so much more, but I don't know."

"You certainly could, and, yes, I would absolutely love to have you," Terk agreed. "But you all should know that I've been talking to Janna about this for years," He turned and looked at the others. "You guys don't understand a couple things here, and it's not my story to tell, but, if she'll give me permission, I will."

When he turned and looked at her, she shrugged. "Sure, why not? It's not as if they don't know everything else."

"Janna was a very influential person, one of the very first social media influencers, so to speak, and it was a great cover for her travels. The government solicited her assistance, so, when she was attacked with the acid, … she was attacked not by a mentally disturbed fan, which is the public line, but by a foreign government agent, who found out that she was working with the US government," he explained, and suddenly it all made sense. "Thus, the US government paid for the bulk of her surgeries. Still, that doesn't begin to cover her pain and suffering and all the time she has spent healing. So, she's never really forgotten nor forgiven them for having led her into something that they had told her would be a completely harmless op."

At that, the others stared at her in surprise.

She shrugged. "Terk doesn't really understand that I'm okay to have walked away from most of that. Sam's birth," her voice choked when she added, "and death changed a lot of things in my life, and I more or less isolated myself from everybody, as you all know by now. Only because this guy here wouldn't stop calling out to me that I came back into the fold, so to speak."

"And that's where you need to stay," Rick stated.

She looked at him. "You're the last one I expected to hear that from."

He gave her a ghost of a smile. "I may have had my doubts at the beginning because I really didn't want to take a novice out into a prison-break op in Russia," he explained, "but you did just fine." As he stared at Janna, he shook his head and added, "Honestly, you did better than fine. And a skill like that, controlling mechanical equipment, … it's something that you need to cultivate, if only to keep yourself safe. I don't know whether it is affected by your emotions, fears, dark thoughts, or nightmares, but I know you deal with all that trauma." Rick gave her a sidelong glance. "Still, that energy gift of yours is definitely something that needs to be protected. Plus, you also need to be in complete control of such a gift."

It was obvious she didn't know what to say.

"At the moment," Royal interjected, "I presume that nobody knows what she did."

"Correct," Terk confirmed, as he glanced around. "You'll all be debriefed, but now you'll come with us. We'll head in to talk to MI6 about this. As Rick described, we need to come up with some plausible cover story as to what happened, and they'll check the vehicles, *blah, blah, blah*, and it will end up being some mechanical error, or it'll be treason or whatever."

He looked around at the others. "I don't care what it is that they want to go with publicly, but it will not involve her name, not again," he stated determinedly. "Janna's been to hell and back over whatever involvement they brought her into in the first place, way back when. However, we do have a decent working relationship with MI6, with Jonas in particular. So, although he won't want to know the details, no way he can avoid it, for obvious reasons." Terk gave them all a crooked smile. "Let's get real. Jonas deals with us frequently, so he already knows that something funky is going on with us, and a huge part of him doesn't want anything to do with it."

"Good," Janna said, her voice faint. "Honestly, I just want to go away and hide for the next half of the century."

"As it turns out, I happen to have a very large castle," Terk shared, "and plenty of space to hide. The biggest advantage is that you can be yourself there. You don't have to worry about our people finding out that you can do these things because they, too, can all do some pretty wild and wonderful things. And, if you wanted to learn some of those tricks, I'm sure there would be no shortage of time and effort available to make that happen. I think you will fit right in, though you'll have to cope with all the babies coming soon, which will no doubt be quite painful to some degree," he added, as an afterthought.

She looked up at him. "You mean, that onslaught of pregnancies you have going on at your place?"

Terk reached out a hand, palm up, and he added, "You're already part of the family. Isn't it time to come home?"

She looked up at him and replied, "I already have a place very close to yours."

"I know that, but I suggest you temporarily stay with us for a while to heal and to get to know everyone. At some point the walls of the castle will burst from overpopulation, and then, if you want to, we'll include your place within the boundaries of the castle," he offered. Terk looked over at Royal. "I presume Royal will be staying too."

She looked at Royal in surprise. "I have no idea."

Royal squeezed her hand. "Yes, you do, and, yes, I will stay, if you'll have me," he told Terk. "A few days or more at the castle to get to know everybody would probably be an excellent idea. Janna has a tendency to want to isolate."

She glared at him.

Terk smiled at that and added, "And that tendency is something we'll work on."

She groaned. "You'll try to turn me into a nice person, won't you?"

"You're already a very nice person," he stated gently. "Just a hurt one. And together, all of us, can fix that."

Her bottom lip trembled, and she pinched it back tightly, almost causing her lip to bleed. He sighed, then looked over at the rest of the gang and asked, "Her ability stays silent and hidden, agreed?"

They all nodded.

"Just like the rest of us," Rick stated. "Still, I would much rather have her on our side than be against her. Plus, we've now got a problem to deal with, the British government."

"Yeah, we sure do," Terk agreed, as he stretched. "But that's okay, it seems to go with the territory. I'll go see if I can get things arranged. Maybe the inquiry and all the debriefing can be moved to the castle."

Royal frowned at him and asked, "Is that really what you want to do? Isn't that bringing the enemy to your door?" He was getting insights that he hadn't expected but now made sense on her ability to navigate metal objects. She was likely sensing mechanical energy on pathways. Machines carried energy, and all movement left energy trails. She probably had no idea how she did what she did, but, by moving energy, she could move … cars.

Terk gave Royal a small smile. "You'll understand more when you're there with us. Having MI6 in our headquarters is not a show of weakness," he said gently. "It's a show of strength, letting them know that they can do nothing to hurt us in our home base," he explained. "Understanding the strength of our own defenses, we can welcome them in, knowing full well that they're not an issue. So it's a pretty-strong chess move."

Royal thought about that and then nodded slowly. "That makes sense." He leaned more heavily against the SUV, feeling his own energy ebb and flow with the strange conversation. "Any chance that we can get moving though? I'm really worried about Bruce."

"That's another reason to move everything to the castle," Terk added, staring at the man whose eyes were now open and looking at them. "Bruce needs to come with us."

She protested. "Are you sure that's fair?"

Terk looked down at her. "And that's the side of this life you don't have any exposure to. It'll be better to bring him to us than to leave him to the traditional doctors who will poke and prod at him, trying to figure out why he's even alive. The reasons he's alive are back at the castle, and the healers need to continue their work. That way Bruce can continue to heal and eventually thrive," Terk shared. "The work is in progress, but it's not that far enough along that we can walk away from the energy healing." Terk turned to Bruce again, addressing him now. "How do you feel about a short holiday in a castle?"

"I would be okay with that," Bruce said cautiously. "I'm not sure about the lack of doctors though."

"Oh, definitely no lack of medical personnel there," Terk corrected. "Even a gynecologist, who keeps getting in my way all the time," he added, with half a smile.

"Hardly an issue for me," Bruce protested, but the others were all grinning.

"Maybe so," Terk agreed, "but let's get you back to the castle, which is still several hours away. Jonas can come, along with the US representative," Terk noted, his tone dry. "And, if they want to bring in the CIA operative, when he arrives, he'll first have to pass my checks before I let him across the moat."

"You really don't like them, do you?" Jonas asked, as he stepped in closer, interrupting their little meeting.

"You know how I feel about the CIA and why," Terk stated, "but they pay well. So, I'll work certain of their assignments, but I'll never trust them," he vowed, his tone deep. "You got any problem with my taking these guys back to the castle, Jonas?"

Jonas hesitated and then shook his head. "At this point, I honestly wouldn't know what else to do with them. Chances are, you'll take them to the hospital, and they'll pronounce them all totally fine, another medical miracle, or else think that we made up all this."

"That could be," Terk agreed. "Some things you're just better off not knowing."

"You mean, like what she did to those vehicles?"

"Did she do anything?" Terk asked, with one eyebrow raised.

Jonas flushed and glared at him. "A part of me really wants to know, and another part of me is like, … hell no. I don't."

"Maybe you should just stick with that *hell no* part," Terk suggested, as he helped Janna to her feet. "These people need rest, and they need a chance to recuperate."

"We still have to talk to them," he warned.

"Yep, and you're welcome to come by tomorrow, after they've had a chance to de-stress, eat, and sleep," he stated with finality. "We'll expect you at what? … Maybe 10:00 a.m.? Can you come that early? Yes, you can," Terk said, with a chuckle. "You're the government. You can make it happen."

And, with that, Janna watched as two more vehicles pulled up. Terk escorted them, nobody making any protests. As soon as Janna had been placed in the back seat of one, Royal climbed in beside her, noting that both Rick and Calum hopped in as well. With the other team in the other vehicle, and Bruce settled as well, they drove away, leaving everybody else standing, staring at them.

She whispered to Calum, "Can we just pull away like that? Without dealing with the repercussions?"

Calum turned and gave her a smile. "There really are some great advantages to being part of Terk's team," he shared. "One, we have a lot of respect from this British government because we do jobs that they can't do, and these jobs we accept always help people," he explained, reaffirming what Royal had hoped. "And," he added, having a laughing fit, "they've learned it's much better to not ask questions, or to block us when we have a plan."

CHAPTER 12

JANNA DOZED, HALF asleep, curled up against Royal's shoulder for the journey. When they took a turn onto a slightly rougher road, which she recognized all too well, she opened her eyes and sat up to see the massive castle looming in the distance. "Well," she murmured, "I'd forgotten how grandiose this place was."

"That's right," Calum noted. "You saw it before we ever bought it, didn't you?"

She nodded. "I considered buying it because I was looking to hide away," she muttered. "But it was really too big for me to take on. Then I was here that day to speak with Terk, to get his help, before we headed out to find you."

"It's really too big for any of us," Rick noted, with a laugh. "Yet we seem to be doing our best to fill it."

She looked at him and nodded. "Yes, you're about to have daughters."

He looked at her in surprise. "Whoa, whoa, whoa, whoa." He was clearly against knowing all that. "None of that. A man gets to have his own personal life, you know? And gets to have some surprises."

"It's not even a surprise," she declared, looking at him. "You already knew."

He burst out laughing. "Oh, you'll have fun when you get settled among us. It might surprise you to realize that you aren't alone and that a lot of people just like you are there."

"That's one of the reasons I would be interested in involving myself with you guys. It's probably the only reason, if I'm honest."

Rick gave a shout of laughter from the front seat. "See? You're really growing on me. And I much prefer that to the hard-ass, stay-away attitude I had to deal with for the whole op."

"Hey, I wasn't hard to deal with," Janna protested. "I just didn't have a whole lot to offer."

"And that was the problem," Rick noted. "You were somebody we dragged along, which will never go down well in my book."

"Yeah, so deal with it," she murmured.

"I did," he said. "And, since it all came out right, we're good. I presume you don't want to go on ops on a regular basis."

"God, no," she muttered. "Leave me at home any day. It really works better for me."

"Good to know," Rick teased. "Considering how much chaos will soon hit us all at home, with all the babies due about the same time, and with you only five minutes up the road, don't be surprised if you get shamed into helping."

"Helping with what?" she asked, looking at him.

"Hell, I don't know, but, if you have any inclination toward kids, we're about to be inundated with a whole pile of them."

"Two are coming fairly quickly," Janna shared. "I wonder if Terk knows."

Calum turned and looked at her. "How quickly?"

She shrugged, just as the other vehicle whipped past them at a speed that was inadvisable at best. "I think it's pretty safe to say very soon"—she pointed—"seeing as how … that's Terk driving, right?" And the vehicle continued to accelerate ahead of them, leaving them all in the dust.

Rick gave a shout and hit the gas pedal. "Wouldn't he let us know?" he asked. "We might be able to help."

She laughed at him. "Ain't nobody going to help right now, guys. This is his wife's job," Janna explained, with a gentle smile. "Besides, the healers are there already. Nothing you can do."

She looked back at Royal. "Expect your energy to drop. Bruce's too," she warned him. "They're all on board helping Celia." She stopped and then asked in confusion, "I don't know where that name came from, but it is Celia, isn't it? Is that the name?"

"Yes," Calum confirmed, looking at her with a nod of approval. "That's Terk's partner."

"Right." Then Janna sighed. "She's been to hell and back too, hasn't she?"

He gave her the gentlest of smiles. "Yes, many of the women have."

"Right. So we all just need to let it go and to start fresh."

"That would be a great idea," he murmured, "for you too."

"Sounds good to me." Then she stopped and looked over at the men, frowning. "*Uh-oh.* So, guys, this has nothing to do with Terk …"

"What?"

"I feel very much like danger's right around the corner."

"Danger for us?" Royal asked Janna. "I'm not getting anything about the pregnancy. … Yet something feels off."

At that warning, Rick, who was driving, turned the wheel of his vehicle hard, and they were flung against the side as he came to a hard stop even as the vehicle still rocked back and forth. Right in front of them appeared a helicopter, landing just out of sight in the trees.

Two people appeared, heading toward them.

Janna thought she recognized them. "Isn't that the two drivers from the kidnapping site?" she whispered, staring at them.

"Yeah," Calum and Rick both affirmed. "Somehow they got ahold of a helicopter and came along. Now the question is, what do they want from us?"

"It ain't good," Royal said, his voice coming out in a gasp. "She's right. My energy is sagging rapidly. Damn, you don't realize how much other people are helping you until they remove the help."

"They're only removing it because they need it for Celia," Janna said, looking at him.

"Oh, I get it," he said. "And, if she needs it, that's where it needs to go. But right now," he whispered, "I won't be any help." And with that he fell back against the seat beside Bruce, and his eyes rolled up into the back of his head, as the lights went out on both of them.

"Shit, shit, shit," she cried out, even as she watched the two men coming toward them.

Her guys didn't have weapons, and she didn't know if it was safe to think that this would be more of a pleasant visit than those previous ones, but she didn't like anything about this. "I can't let them take Royal or Bruce," she cried out.

"Easy," Rick muttered, "let's figure out what's going on first."

"What, and let them shoot us?"

He looked at her and added, "I put up a guard. Just calm down."

She nodded slowly, her breath coming out in rapid puffs, as the two men approached them.

After the men withdrew handcuffs, they ordered everyone to step out of the vehicle.

She looked at Rick and asked, “Yeah, now what?”

“Now we’ll get out,” Rick replied.

Calum and Riff got out and stepped up to the men and stared. “What’s the problem?”

A conversation was had that she couldn’t hear and wasn’t even sure what language it was in.

Rick looked at her. “You got any ideas?”

“Yeah, sure. How about I just blast them into tomorrow?”

He gave a snort. “How about something a whole lot less violent?”

“Royal is the one who could do that.” She reached over and gave Royal a nudge and sensed energy swirling around on the inside of the vehicle. “I think he already is.”

She watched as Calum appeared to have some sort of confused conversation with the two men, but he returned to the vehicle, leaving Riff to continue talks with the two men.

Calum kept his voice low as he explained, “I’m not sure what is going on. They’re arguing about just getting back into the helicopter and leaving, but they first wanted to take us with them. They keep changing their minds and are going back and forth. I don’t know what the hell is going on.”

“It’s Royal,” she piped up. “Even though he’s out for the count—or maybe he’s out because of this energy work—he’s trying to affect their decision-making.”

“In that case we need to give him energy so he can fully do this,” Rick stated, laying a hand on Royal’s shin. A snap of energy filled the vehicle. Then Calum added his hand to

Royal's knee as well, and, linked like that, they surged more and more energy into Royal. Even as they watched the energy flow visible in the vehicle, they kept an eye on the men outside, talking to Riff, who appeared to come to a final decision and, with a nod, those two men got back into the helicopter.

"Please tell me that I shouldn't crash that helicopter," she murmured, "because that's what I want to do."

"We only crash things if we have to," Rick stated. "I'm not sure what all that was about. It seemed to be mixed messages all around."

"I suspect that's Royal attempting to help but getting in the way."

"What's to stop them from coming back?"

"That depends on where they're going and what they're supposed to be doing right now because, if they go home without their prisoners," Rick stated, his tone hard, even as she could see energy pulse stronger and stronger into Royal's leg, "they will have their own problems to deal with."

"Right," Janna agreed. "I guess blowing up the helicopter won't help, will it?"

"No, it won't, and the Russians might take it the wrong way."

"What if it blew up on the way back to London?"

At that, both men turned and looked at her. "Can you do that?"

"I don't know." She gave a harsh laugh. "But to keep Royal safe, all of us safe," she added, "I would definitely try my hardest."

Rick smiled at her. "We appreciate the warrior attitude, but we're not trying to start a war with another country, and, as long as these two guys leave us alone right now, we will leave them alone."

"Fine," she muttered, as the helicopter slowly lifted into the air and flew away. She let out a hard breath and looked over to see Royal's eyes open, staring at her. "Nice job," she said gently. "We really do need to talk."

He gave a ghost of a smile. "Yeah, but in order to have that happen, I really need some rest."

And, with that, he closed his eyes and fell asleep.

ROYAL WOKE UP again as they pulled up into the long driveway before the huge castle looming ahead.

He stared at it, then looked over at her. "I just figured it out. No way you could make a whole vehicle move, so you just use a metal part, as a conductor of energy. You focused your energy on the metal accelerator pedal."

She gave him a ghost of a smile and then a clipped nod as they all got out and headed for the huge front entrance to the castle. "Yes, that is the gist of it." The other men stared at her, then shook their heads and kept on walking. "Is that wrong?"

"No, not at all," Royal said. "I was trying to figure it out because it's not as if energy travels wildly for no reason, and for you to get the vehicles themselves moving is a whole different deal. However, because metal is a conductor, focusing on one essential metal part makes a whole lot more sense." Royal grinned, pleased at having figured that out.

"It was important to you to figure it out, wasn't it?"

He laughed. "I just wanted to understand it. I'm sure these guys do too."

She shrugged. "It's just basic mechanics."

"I know, and that's the genius part of it," he said, with a delighted smile.

They were still talking about it as they walked up to the front of the castle. When they entered, they were met with complete silence.

Janna was prepared for it. "Remember how fast Terk was driving when he raced ahead of us?"

At that, the men looked around, and Rick got an odd look in his gaze. He looked over at Calum and said in a panic, "I'll be back in a minute." With that, he quickly disappeared.

Calum walked into the huge kitchen and announced, "I'm putting on some coffee, and then we'll show you guys to your rooms."

"Are you sure you have rooms for us?" Janna asked. "I know this place is massive, but it needed a ton of work, from what I can remember."

"We've done nothing but work on it," Calum replied. "Sometimes getting away on missions is nice because we can escape the noise for a bit."

She nodded and smiled at that. "I couldn't imagine living among all that noise and disarray. I absolutely loved this castle, but the whole scope of things was a bit too much for me."

"And that's good," Calum said, "because that left it available for us."

She sat down at the table, looked over at a still very exhausted Royal. "Will you make it?"

"I will, but I do need to crash soon." He looked ghostly. "I see you had people take Bruce inside but I really want to check up on him."

"Rick's probably gone to see where everybody's at and

what's going on, although I could have told him without his having to do that."

"Tell me what?" Rick asked, as he rejoined them.

"That Celia's gone into labor," Janna replied, "but it's too early."

He looked at her and frowned, "Are you sure it's too early?"

She nodded. "It's … it's not that it's too early because she's got multiple births, so maybe that's what I'm getting."

"Yes, she's carrying multiples," Rick confirmed. "Almost everybody here is."

She frowned at him.

He nodded. "It must have something to do with the energy. Nobody was particularly aware of the cumulative effect of how energy works when we're all together with partners, who have their own energy skills," he explained, giving her a crooked grin.

"Wow," she murmured. "That must have been a shock."

"It absolutely was, a good one in many ways, but it's the second time around that we should be incredibly careful about."

Janna started to giggle.

He glared at her and muttered, "It's not funny."

"It's absolutely hilarious," she said, "because that is funny, you must admit, and more so that I'm not part of it." And then she laughed again.

"Unless you want to be part of it," he noted with a pointed look.

She sighed. "I don't know if I could go through that again."

"A heart condition is not guaranteed to happen with a second one," he pointed out. "In fact, it's quite rare to repeat within siblings, I'd think."

"It is rare," she agreed, "but, once you've lost one, … it's so hard to even think about going through that again, knowing you could lose another one."

"Yet you wouldn't be alone this time," Rick noted. "And I'm sure that could make all the difference in the world."

"It sure could," she muttered. "I don't know. I'll, … I'll see. I'm definitely not at that stage just yet."

At that, he frowned at her. "None of us were either. But the more you hang around this place, that energy just seems to fly through the air."

She started to laugh and laugh. "And that's the thing about being part of a community. *A*, we get to talk about this and realize that it is something that needs to be discussed, and, *B*, there is that knock-on effect, isn't there?"

"Absolutely," Rick confirmed.

Just then Terk walked into the kitchen, looking a little more ragged than she'd seen him before. She gave him a big grin. "How is the soon-to-be-daddy doing?"

He sighed. "She's not necessarily in labor right now," he shared cautiously.

"No, and it's pretty early. I was saying that to them just now. It seems to be too early, but then I realized you're dealing with multiple births, so, in that case, it's not so early."

He nodded. "We're still waiting to see whether this is false labor or not," he added. "I just don't understand how this isn't something the body can just turn around and do."

"Oh, the body can absolutely turn around and do it, and does," Janna stated, again with a chuckle. "But it also does it in its own timeframe, not yours. You're used to controlling everything, and this is something you'll have to let go of and just let it be. Some things you simply cannot control."

His lips quirked. "Yeah, so I've been told."

She burst out laughing. "A time for you and a time for her, and definitely it's a special time for both of you." Janna nodded. "But this is definitely something that the babies and her body get to control, not you."

"On that note, let's get you up to your rooms, so Royal can crash. He looks more than a little worse for the wear."

"Yeah, he's pretty tired," she muttered, "but we do need to bring you up to date on the Russians and the helo…" It took more than a moment but when done and, with Terk's help, Royal got to his feet, and they moved him over to an elevator.

She looked at it and asked curiously, "There wasn't an elevator here before."

"No, and it's one of those things that we put in fairly quickly, once we realized we had all these rather large bellies happening," Terk shared, with a sigh. "It was supposed to be a development for a year down the road, but …"

She flashed him a big grin. "Smart decision," she said, with a cheeky smile as they went up.

He led them to a door at the far end of the hallway.

"You sure you've got room for us right now?" Janna asked.

"We sure do, and, until this guy is back on his feet, I wouldn't suggest you hurry off on your own."

"Right, he needs rest," she agreed, "and, if your healers have anything to share about the healing or some tips that I can use to help him, I would appreciate it."

"We'll get into that discussion as soon as we get an assessment on Bruce, which is happening right now, while Celia's contractions have calmed down," he told her. "I guess we'll need to get some training system in place. I've just realized that we may not have enough healers."

"Yet it must be enough," Janna noted calmly, squeezing his hand. "Just because you think you always have enough energy, it's really channelers that you need."

He looked at her and then flashed a big grin. "See? That's exactly what we need. … More people who really understand energy."

"Yeah."

"Hey, I finally figured out how she made those vehicles jump forward," Royal told Terk, with a half chuckle. "Believe me that made me feel a whole lot better."

"You mean, using her energy to conduct a metal part?" Terk asked, with an eyebrow raised.

"Yeah." Royal sighed. "I didn't get that at first. Metal is a conductor, and her affinity with metal is how she can motivate it."

"Yep, and nobody ever sees it that way, but it's one of the easiest things to bend to your will," Terk noted. "And it's not even so much about bending it to your will as it's a superhighway to do what you need to do. I'm just glad she thought of it."

"Me too," Janna muttered.

They walked into a small apartment, self-contained, and she looked around in admiration. "Wow, you guys have really done a lot of work here."

"We had quite a bit of help in the beginning, getting things organized," Terk said. "And I admit, some people still come back and forth to give us a hand to sort this out, as we work on new projects," he murmured. "But, for the most part, we've now got several guest apartments. Plus, we're always finishing up new apartments for new people, so this one is yours for the time being." He helped Royal lay down on the bed and frowned at him.

"I'm fine," Royal said. "Go on. I'll be okay. If I get coffee when I wake up and food and a shower later, I think I'll be feeling a ton better."

"Yeah, you can have all that," Terk said. "This apartment should be stocked, ready for you, but we might need to grab you some towels downstairs. Coffee's downstairs too." Terk turned and looked at Janna, and she nodded.

"I'll come back down with you and grab some, but I want him to sleep first."

Royal smiled at her. "As long as you come right back, that's not a problem. I'll just stay right here and crash. I am done in." And, much to her amazement, he closed his eyes, and, within seconds, they heard his deep, calm breathing.

CHAPTER 13

"I DON'T UNDERSTAND how he can do that," Janna muttered, "but then he seems to have that ability. It's as if he could just ease out of consciousness and into this altered state."

"It goes along with energy work, I think," Terk replied, as he led the way back down to the kitchen. "If you want to grab some towels, some are in there." He pointed to a large closet. "Cleaning supplies are in here, and, as far as your living quarters are concerned, you're on your own for keeping up your apartment, however you want it." He laughed. "We don't even begin to have enough staff for that housekeeping stuff. If you want to grab a nap yourself, go right ahead."

She nodded. "I did want some coffee and to see if I could snatch a laptop or something. Otherwise I can pop over to my place and grab one."

"If you want to make that trip, you can. I can give you a set of wheels or give you a lift."

She pondered that. "I need clothes anyway, so I'll go," she muttered. "Maybe I'll just take a vehicle, if you've got mine accessible, seeing as how I left it here. Since he's sleeping, I should slip out now."

"But how are you doing for exhaustion?"

"I'm doing okay." She shrugged. "I just want to ensure I

get back before he is up."

"Are you sure you don't want somebody to go with you?"

She looked at him. "Why? We're not meeting with MI6 until 10:00 a.m. tomorrow, correct?"

He nodded. "That's correct."

"Good enough," she said.

He led her to the garage and pointed out her small car and handed her the keys. She got into her vehicle, tired and yet wanting this errand over with, she knew she would feel better with some clean clothes and a laptop, and pulled out from the castle and headed home again.

Just getting home and walking inside filled her with a sense of freedom. She'd set out to save Royal, and she'd managed it in a big way. Feeling that wonderful sense of homecoming, she headed up to her bedroom and quickly packed up enough clothing for several days. She didn't want to stay too long at Terk's castle, not when she had her own private space here, but there was definitely a need to keep both Bruce and Royal at the castle, where the healing could take place at a stronger level.

Plus, she definitely didn't want to bring MI6 here. Even though they undoubtedly knew where she lived and who she was, she wanted to keep them completely out of her personal life, as much as she could. Deciding on a quick shower, she quickly hopped in, scrubbed down, then dried off and put on fresh clothes. She dumped her dirty clothes into the laundry, grabbed a toothbrush and a few other essentials, adding them to the things she'd already packed.

As she walked back down to her main entrance, she looked around to see if she was missing anything else and then froze. Standing in front of her was one of the two men who had been on the helicopter. She let her breath out in a harsh rush of air. "What are you doing in my house?" she snapped.

He just smiled, a lazy smile that set her heart on edge. "Nice to know this is where you live," he said menacingly, "and you're all alone too."

She narrowed her gaze at him. "And? What's that got to do with you?"

"Oh, I think I owe you for making me look stupid and getting me in trouble with my bosses."

"You didn't even have time to go home and come back again," she muttered.

"No, we already got our marching orders," he stated, with a harsh laugh. "Turns out they are … very cut-and-dried. No going back." He walked around, looking at her place, and then turned, as if he needed to get something out of his system. "That means I can't go home to a job that paid well and kept my head held high with pride," he murmured. "So, I decided to have a little visit with the one who was so obviously at the root of my problem," he said, glaring at her. "You didn't have to do that."

"Really?" she asked, staring at him warily, as he looked around her small space. It was anything but small by any measure, but she was feeling backed into a corner. Why had she come here alone? Terk had even offered to drive her himself.

Royal wasn't here to help her out this time, so there was no chance to trigger a wishy-washy mind-set, at least not long enough to get this guy taken care of. She sent out a warning to the ethers, hoping that somebody, Terk even, could send help or backup of some sort, maybe even wake up Royal and have him hopefully confuse this guy enough to change his mind.

At this point, she would take anything. The last thing she wanted was to end up dead, shot in her own place, because she had thought to come get clean clothes. That would be an irony far too hard to accept. "So, what's your plan?" she asked, as she tossed her backpack over one shoulder. "Presumably you brought wheels."

"Of course," he said.

"And your friend?'

"He's gone back to face the music, but I … will not go back in defeat." He was starting to bubble in anger, and she could see it in his aura. "I will only go back with the job completed."

"Ah, so you're planning on taking me all the way back to Moscow, is that it?"

He nodded. "That is the only way to restore my honor."

"Your honor won't get restored, no matter what," she muttered, staring at him. "You really can't figure that out yet?"

Fury flashed across his face, and she realized that, once again, her casual seat-of-her-pants style would get her in trouble.

She asked him, "How is it that you think none of my friends will be there to help?"

He looked around and smiled. "They think the danger is past. They think it's over with," he stated, "so it really doesn't have anything to do with them now. This is all about you and me and how you made me look like a fool," he growled.

"What is it you think I did?" she asked. "You were in the driver's seat of a vehicle. I have no idea what happened, but you killed your own man. I just figured that somebody paid you off to be a traitor to your own country."

His face lit with almost an unworldly air as he stared at her. "No. It was you. We heard stories about all of you, but the only one who could have done it was you. *You* did it."

She shook her head at that. "I don't know how you figure that," she argued, trying to come up with a game plan that would work. "That's all BS." He frowned at her. "Here you are blaming a woman, when I'm sure your bosses would never begin to think that such a thing could be possible to begin with, especially by a woman."

He shook his head. "It doesn't matter. You're the one I take."

"Ah, so it doesn't really matter if I did the damage or not, but you think I'm the weakest link? I'm the one you think you can just pick up and carry back, as if a head on a stick, so to speak. So, I am just to be a trophy for them, some bargaining chip for you to save your job, and for them to use against the government? That's it, *huh*?"

He nodded, with a smile. "You will do." He gave a hysterical laugh. "And the men? The men you came to help? They will want to rescue you, so, yes, you will definitely do nicely."

She winced at that because, of course, if Royal had any idea where she was, no way he wouldn't come after her. "That's nice, but you've already injured those men so much that it's not as if they can help."

"Yes, but eventually they will. They'll pressure their government, and my government will be happy to have that bargaining chip," he stated. "So, get going. Come on. Out the door."

She groaned but steadily walked out the front door, and, as she did, she found Royal standing on the other side,

Calum half holding him up.

She raced forward. "What are you doing?" she cried out. "I left you sound asleep."

"Yeah, but you left," Royal said, "and I could sense the wrongness."

"It would have been nice if you'd mentioned something beforehand," she said, with a mock smile, "because this guy was waiting for me when I came downstairs."

Calum eyed the man in confusion. "Wow. Are you sure you want to do this?"

The other man growled. "She must come back with me. Failure is not allowed. My life is over, but if I take her—"

"Your life is already over," Royal declared. "You may have had some freedom and made a new life somewhere if you'd just disappeared, but now you've tried to kidnap a British citizen in her own home. Do you really think that'll go over well?"

He shrugged. "It doesn't matter. If I don't succeed, I might as well die trying."

Calum gave a sad sigh. "That's fine with me, good even, but the British government feels differently."

"Why do you say that?" he asked.

"Because we've already talked to Jonas, and they want you alive."

"No, I won't be taken alive."

"You won't take her or us out of here, so I'm not sure what you think your options are."

The man frowned at him and pulled out a gun. "Did you think I wasn't armed?"

"No," Calum said. "I just don't care."

The Russian stared at him in shock. "I don't understand. How is this even possible? How can you people be so calm in the face of certain death?" He took a step forward, lifting the weapon higher and pointing it at them. "If she doesn't come with me alive, I will kill all of you and take pictures," he declared, with a nod. "That will make my country happy and will redeem my position."

"Maybe, but it won't make anybody else happy," Calum said, with that same lackadaisical tone.

She smiled at Calum and pointed to Royal. "Royal is about to collapse."

Calum asked Royal, "Are you okay?"

"Yeah, I'm fine. Now that we're here, and she's safe, I'm feeling much better."

"She's not safe. You are fools," the Russian cried out in fury. "How dare you ignore me?" He stomped around as he bellowed, then stepped forward, ready to fire the weapon at her.

She looked over at Calum. "So, is this something you want to handle, or do you prefer I take care of it myself?"

Calum chuckled. "You've had all the fun so far, so I'll take care of this one."

He took several quick steps forward and, in a surprise move, pivoted and kicked backward, up and high, hitting the Russian hard in the jaw.

The Russian stared at him blankly, then slowly slid to the ground.

"Ooh, I love that move," Janna said. "How very primitive of you."

He didn't seem to mind her mocking tone, and, besides, he got his man. "What can I say? There are times," Calum said, looking down at the unconscious man as he picked up the weapon, "when a little physical violence feels pretty good."

"Yeah, I get that. I wanted to kick him myself."

He flashed her a grin. "You've already pretty well taken everything else from him, so really no point."

She laughed and asked, "Now what?"

"Now we'll phone MI6, and Jonas will come and collect him." Calum looked around her place. "I will stay here and wait for Jonas. Meanwhile, you can take lover boy here back to our place, get him settled into your apartment, but maybe this time stay with him, so he actually stays put and gets some rest?"

She glared at Royal. "Did you hear that? You need to get back to bed and stay there."

He gave her a crooked grin. "Yeah, but will you stay with me?"

She flushed. "Maybe, if you will behave yourself."

"Not happening," he said, as he looped an arm over her shoulders. "But it might be a day or two before I can do anything other than sleep."

It took no small amount of effort and muscle, but she finally got him to the car and, with Calum's help, into the vehicle.

Calum added, "I'll phone ahead. Just get him back to the house, and they'll get him upstairs again."

And he was right. By the time she drove into the yard at the castle, several men were waiting. They quickly picked up Royal and disappeared with him.

She got out more slowly, only to find Terk standing there, his hands on his hips.

"That's one of the reasons why we generally go everywhere as part of a team."

"Maybe so," she admitted, "but I honestly didn't think the Russians had anything left to care about."

"Never forget what it's like for these guys in some of these countries or organizations when they fail," Terk noted. "There's always a backlash, and they end up somewhat desperate, with nothing left to lose, which is when they are the most dangerous."

"Hopefully this time he's in good hands, and the backlash is truly over with, and we can now relax."

"I hope so," Terk said cheerfully, "but we'll be on alert anyway. I'm very sorry that happened, Janna. I should have insisted you take someone along."

"You are distracted today, and who wouldn't be?"

He then waved her upstairs. "Go on up and take care of Royal, and try to get some rest yourself."

She nodded. "I will, but I'll grab that coffee on the way." She picked up coffee and made her way up to the apartment. As she got inside, she found Royal nearly asleep, but not quite, clearly waiting for her. She walked over, dropped her backpack on the floor and set the coffee on the bedside table. She sat on the bed beside Royal and patted his cheek. "Go on now. Get some sleep."

He stared up at her. "Will you stay?"

"I promise. I'll stay."

He closed his eyes and whispered, "Thank you." And, with that, he crashed.

She sat stretched out on the bed beside him, then opened up her laptop and proceeded to spend a few hours catching up on the world that she had left behind, before starting this venture. Periodically she stopped to spend a few moments wondering what she would have done if Calum and Royal hadn't shown up at her house.

If they didn't have a system already in place to deal with these things, then it would have been so different for her.

Sure, she'd gotten into trouble because of the original plan, but she wasn't so foolish as to think that it couldn't happen again and again. She had to admit to enjoying having people to count on for help, something she hadn't allowed herself for a very long time.

She was also enjoying interacting with people, something she was frankly surprised at and out of practice with, realizing she needed to curb her sharp tongue if she would share this home with so many people. The benefits of joining Terk and his band of merry men definitely far outweighed the cons at the moment, and she found herself looking forward to meeting the rest of them, especially the women.

Now all she had to do was get this guy back on his feet and ensure Bruce would be okay, and then maybe she would see a way forward. As soon as her now cold coffee was gone, she curled up right beside Royal and slept.

ROYAL WOKE UP and yet remained silent and still, as he tried to figure out where he was and what had happened. As the memories filtered back in, he looked over to see Janna curled up beside him. As she promised, she had stuck around and stayed at his side. He reached out a hand and gently shifted the still damp hair back off her face, realizing that she must have grabbed a shower somewhere along the line, something he could really use himself.

He just wasn't sure where his energy level was at.

Still, determined to follow through, he slowly sat up, walked to the bathroom, and used the facilities, then took a good look at his face. Yeah, a shower was something he most definitely needed. He turned on the water, then moving carefully and slowly, had a hot shower. When he came back out, despite the longer hair and beard he hadn't been able to cut all this time, he was looking clean at least, though very thin, pale, and a bit scraggly. He found Janna sitting up in bed and waiting for him.

She smiled. "You look much better."

"I feel better," he acknowledged, "but, at some point, I'll need to get some shaving stuff."

"Sorry, I never even thought of that," she said. "It'll be on the list to get when we have a few minutes. You're in desperate need of clothes as well, though Terk told me that they have some basics they keep in stock, since they frequently get surprise visitors."

"I can work with that, as long as you don't mind a beard," he added, with a chuckle.

"If it's yours, I don't mind a bit." She opened up her arms, and he sat back down on the bed and gave her a big hug. "How are you feeling?" she asked, eyeing him critically.

"I'm fine. I feel better. Obviously it'll be a few days before I get some energy back, and then months of putting on some weight and building muscle again, but I'm on the mend. Have you had an update on Bruce?" he asked anxiously.

"Not recently, no, and I just woke up myself."

"Right. So, we do need to check on him."

"We do, yet I think the others have it firmly in hand." She stroked his cheek. "I really want to learn how to do what they do—the healing, I mean. Apparently the twins are quite skilled at it."

"It sure seems so. It's nothing short of a miracle that Bruce is still with us," Royal said, with a gentle smile. "But honestly, considering the abilities you already have, I'm sure you'll take to it easily."

"I don't know about that, but I would like a chance to find out."

"Does that mean you've decided you want to align with Terk?" he asked.

She nodded. "Yes, and, if nothing else, I saw the benefits all over again after having them handle the problem at my place," she muttered. "It was nice not to be alone. Plus, they took care of dealing with the government and all that crap."

"Yeah, it was great we could just come straight back here."

"Of course we've got that whole debriefing mess with MI6 to deal with tomorrow," she reminded him, "and we can't get out of it. Still, it will be nice to know that, once again, no matter what, we're not alone."

He nodded. "I've been thinking of that aspect myself. Definitely some advantages to being part of a team."

"What about you though?" she asked. "Are you even free to leave the government?"

"Oh, yes. I won't be working for them anymore. I wasn't planning on it after this job anyway. I'd already made up my mind that I was coming back to find you. Then it all turned to crap, and I found myself tortured and starved, stuck in a Russian prison."

She gave him a gentle smile, then kissed him. "I spoke to Bruce briefly, and he mentioned that you told him all about me."

"Absolutely." Royal chuckled. "When you think you won't survive, you focus on all the things you've missed out on. Things that you should have done, that you could have done, and *you* were at the top of my regrets list. So, I'm very grateful to have a second chance." Then he wrapped her up in another big hug.

She smiled. "Even though I didn't … te Sam?"

"Yes. … Obviously I would have liked to hav him and to have been there for you through all that pain," he said, with a glassy gaze. "I would have liked to meet my, … my son," he whispered gently. "There are enough things in life we must deal with, without adding more, especially those we can do nothing about," he murmured. "It's definitely time to let some of this go." Then he tilted her chin and kissed her gently.

When he pulled back ever-so-slightly, her eyes were crossed, and she gasped. "God. Everything just seems to be so much *more* with you."

"I think it's the energy, and now that you mention it," he murmured, "you pack quite a punch yourself."

She smiled at him. "What about the fact that everybody here seems to have this whole pregnancy thing going on?"

He hesitated, then looked at her and asked, "How do you feel about trying again?"

"It's not so much about *trying* again," she noted, "as I'm pretty sure I would have no problem getting pregnant, but that whole journey? … Well, doing it alone was pretty rough."

"I wouldn't want you doing it alone," he muttered, tapping her on the nose. "But being here, there is a good chance that, unless we can figure out how that energy can be stopped, you'll end up in that state."

She gave him a beautiful smile. "I'm not at all upset about that. I always wanted a family. But, after everything, I guess I just never thought it would happen to me."

He nodded, then kissed the scar on her face in that same

gentle way he'd done before, letting her know that it made absolutely no difference to him. "I suggest we let Mother Nature take its course."

She laughed. "Maybe once or twice, but we won't let it continue until we have a whole baseball team. We'll draw the line somewhere."

He burst out laughing. "Agreed, but two would be nice. Two would be very nice. And, by the way," he said, as he waggled his eyebrows, "I'm feeling much better, so absolutely no point in wasting time. We might as well get started on that plan."

She burst out laughing, then wrapped her arms around his neck and held him close. She already felt the evidence of his need against her belly. "You know you should rest, right?"

"Nope, not happening. This is more restoring than any rest could possibly give me," he whispered against her hair, as he kissed his way down her neck, her throat, and behind her ears, gently leaving a trail of nerve endings waking up slowly, as if they'd been asleep for a very long time. "You're very special, and I'm so grateful to be here with you, so grateful for everything you did to bring me back."

She tapped a finger over his lips and whispered, "And yet it better not be gratitude that has you here right now," she murmured.

"Nope. Never. It's love. It's pure, unadulterated love. Let me show you."

And, with that, he went to town, showing her by his actions, his words, and the break in his voice as he spoke about how much he cared and how much he thought about her, as he trailed kisses up and down her body and explored every inch of her, until she was crying out with need.

When he finally slipped inside her, he whispered, "Now *this* is where home is."

She exploded moments later, her body a wealth of nerve endings, but more than that, her heart fully opened for the first time in a very long while. She had to agree with him. This was home.

She welcomed him back into her life and into her heart, whispering, "You'll never leave me, right?"

"I'll never leave," he vowed. "Not now, not tomorrow, not ever, I promise. What we have isn't temporary. This is forever."

And he kissed her again.

EPILOGUE

TWO DAYS LATER, early in the morning, Terk sat in the kitchen, his head in his hands, when his phone rang. Sophia came in, putting the call up on the TV. He looked at her in surprise.

"It's Levi."

He nodded, as he looked up at the big screen. "Levi, how're you doing?"

Levi opened his mouth to speak and then frowned. "Are you guys okay?"

"Yeah, it's been a hell of a few days," Terk muttered. "It seems as if Celia's in pre-labor, then she's not, then she is. Man, I, for one, find it more than a little frustrating."

Levi laughed. "Yeah, and, for Celia, it's ten times worse. This is definitely a new experience for you, isn't it?"

"Absolutely," he muttered, almost with a groan. "We're all waiting and excited and worried and trepidatious and every emotion in between. But our last job finished successfully, and things are calming down, although it was a little on the rough side." Terk sighed. "We rescued two Americans, and now we're all just trying to recuperate."

"So, I hear you have Bruce over there."

"Yeah, so what do you know about Bruce? He's had a rough go and is still in and out of it. He's unconscious or close to it a good share of the time still, though he is improving."

"But he'll make it, right?" Ice asked, her face coming into view.

Terk smiled broadly when he saw her. "Hey, Ice. You get kudos from me on having kids. I'm, … I'm still struggling, and the babies aren't even here yet. And it's only our first time."

She burst out laughing. "Yep, there is nothing quite like it," she murmured. "I would love to chat on that, and we will sometime soon, but back to Bruce. What's going on?"

"He's okay. He's just … it'll take some time. We used so much energy to keep him alive as we worked to get him here that we can't really put him into standard medical care. They would never understand what they were looking at, and we need him close by to keep up the energy treatments. I am sure that he'll make it, but it'll take him a while. He was mistreated terribly, and frankly it's a miracle he survived. Without help from Royal during their captivity, Bruce wouldn't have made it. I'm sure of it."

"His prognosis is good to know," Ice told Terk, as she looked over at Levi pointedly. "I guess you didn't get a chance to tell him, did you?"

Levi shook his head, and then another face appeared on the screen.

Terk studied the other woman, feeling a stirring deep inside. "Taryn?" he asked, after a moment.

She gave him a bright smile. "Hey, somehow I found my way to Levi's."

"That's an interesting place for you," Terk noted.

"After leaving England the way I did, not too sure what I wanted to do next, it just seemed right that this is where I landed."

"Anyway, Terk, I gather she's one of yours," Levi stated, with one of those long-suffering sighs. "Seems as if every time I find somebody new and interesting, almost immediately I find out they're one of yours."

"Oh, absolutely. Taryn and I did a couple jobs together way back when, before I started working exclusively with this team," Terk explained to Levi and then looked at her. "I had no idea you were over there."

"After I lost my partner," she began, "I went AWOL for a while. A long while." She gave him a lopsided grin. "But it's all good now."

He nodded in understanding. "That'll do it, won't it?"

"It absolutely will," she stated, then changed her tone to all business. "I understand from Levi that you've had a lot of changes in your world."

He gave her a bright grin. "Yes, and even more in the next day or so, but you guys had a particular reason for calling, I'm sure."

Levi nodded. "Yeah. Taryn brought somebody with her. Another young woman, Amara, who apparently was looking for Bruce."

Terk frowned at that. "If that's the case, she'll be happy to know that Bruce is here."

"She's not sure whether it's him or not, so that just adds to her worry."

Terk laughed. "It should be easy enough to identify him, once we send over some photos."

"That would help," Levi said. "Also Amara says that Bruce is special."

"I would agree, based on what Royal has shared with me. However, Bruce hasn't exactly been conscious enough to let us know just how special he may be, though."

"She says he definitely has abilities."

"That wouldn't surprise me," Terk stated, with a note of humor. "Yet we have no idea about his skills to date. We're just trying to keep him alive. He's out cold most of the time, occasionally surfacing for a matter of moments, but he's mostly just out."

Levi nodded at that. "Amara's asking your permission to come over and see him."

"Permission granted," Terk replied cautiously, "though it would help to know whether she's friend or foe first."

At that, another woman stepped into the visual frame. "Friend, very close friend," Amara added, "at least I hope so. I haven't seen Bruce in many years."

"Right. And why do you want to see him now?" Terk asked cautiously, studying her, trying to get a better handle on her energy.

She whispered, "Because I care. I kept getting all these messages, saying that he was hurt. By way of Taryn, we came to Levi, and, through Levi and Ice, now we're coming to you."

"Bruce is here. He is hurt. I'm hoping he'll make it. It's pretty touch-and-go at times," Terk shared, "but you're welcome to come see him." He then looked at Taryn. "Are you coming too?"

She hesitated, then shook her head. "I was hoping that maybe you had somebody over there you could send to help us here, or at least maybe run a ground crew."

"What's the matter?" Terk asked.

"I got wind of a few children being held hostage by a man here in Texas," she began in a tone that made him curious. "And these children, I believe, are gifted."

"He's holding them hostage? Why?"

"Because he wants to sell them to the highest bidder," she stated, her tone harsh.

Terk winced. "*Great*, that's exactly what we need, isn't it?"

"Levi can supply one or two men, and I was hoping that I could get some help from your side."

"For people like us, always, you know that."

She smiled. "Just checking that things are still the same as they were before."

"That will never change," Terk declared. "And you always know that, if you need something from me, you can contact me, without any reservations. So, if this one is happening in Levi's corner of the world, I'm grateful. Things are kind of chaotic here at the moment."

She laughed. "Yet you'll be very happy in another day."

He perked up at that. "I sure hope you're right about that *another day* thing."

"I am. We'll keep in touch, but I do know that we'll need some assistance."

"Okay. Do you have any idea who and what's going on over there?"

"I've heard kids are involved."

"Does the kidnapper have any biological claim over them?"

"He's the uncle," she said, then hesitated.

"And it has been confirmed that the children are gifted?" he asked Taryn.

She replied with a question. "Do you remember my talents?"

He dredged up the memories in the back of his head. "Yes. Is that how you found these kids?"

She nodded. "Yes."

Terk knew someone else who could sense psychic abilities in people too, just like Taryn. Might be a good person for this job, if Alex was willing. He'd spent so much time in VA clinics, looking for those he could help, that he might not be interested. Then again he'd mentioned getting burnt out. Mentally Terk sent off a message to Alex, as Taryn filled Terk in further.

"They're his sister-in-law's kids. She's dead. The uncle lost track of the family, when the kids' father disappeared after their mother's death—just went crazy and left, abandoning his own children. Because they're biologically related to the uncle, I highly suspect that the uncle is correct in thinking that they do have abilities. And, of course, he's just being the usual asshole, trying to get something out of it transactionally."

"That's something we'll put a stop to."

She hesitated. "If need be, I'm prepared to buy them."

Terk sucked in his breath. "That would not be a precedent we want to set."

"Maybe not, but neither can I take a chance on losing them. Let me know whatever you decide, and I'll keep in touch."

And, with that, she ended the call, and the screen went blank.

This concludes Book 9 of Terk's Guardians: Royal.

Read about Alex: Terk's Guardians, Book 10

Terk's Guardians: Alex (Book #10)

Born with the ability to see psychic abilities in others, Alex finds himself called to help out a mutual friend, someone with similar abilities to Alex's. Plus this mutual friend is on a mission to save innocent children. No way Alex can say no to that.

Taryn is desperate to save two children—both with abilities—from a greedy family member. Taryn needs help, so she contacted Levi, looking to see if he had men to spare. Of course that took her to Terk, with a similar request. In Taryn's world, anyone with similar talents who needs help gets it. Period. Finding out these children were being exploited by their uncle made it doubly hard.

But the uncle looking for an easy way to profit off these gifted children isn't willing to step aside, … not without taking down everyone around him …

Find Book 10 here!

To find out more visit Dale Mayer's website.

https://geni.us/DMSAlex

Author's Note

Thank you for reading Royal: Terk's Guardians, Book 9! If you enjoyed the book, please take a moment and leave a short review.

Dear reader,

I love to hear from readers, and you can contact me at my website: www.dalemayer.com or at my Facebook author page. To be informed of new releases and special offers, sign up for my newsletter or follow me on BookBub. And if you are interested in joining Dale Mayer's Reader Group, here is the Facebook sign up page.
http://geni.us/DaleMayerFBGroup

Cheers,
Dale Mayer

About the Author

Dale Mayer is a *USA Today* best-selling author, best known for her SEALs military romances, her Psychic Visions series, and her Lovely Lethal Garden cozy series. Her contemporary romances are raw and full of passion and emotion (Broken But … Mending, Hathaway House series). Her thrillers will keep you guessing (Kate Morgan, By Death series), and her romantic comedies will keep you giggling (*It's a Dog's Life*, a stand-alone novella; and the Broken Protocols series, starring Charming Marvin, the cat).

Dale honors the stories that come to her—and some of them are crazy, break all the rules and cross multiple genres!

To go with her fiction, she also writes nonfiction in many different fields, with books available on résumé writing, companion gardening, and the US mortgage system. All her books are available in print and ebook format.

Connect with Dale Mayer Online

Dale's Website – www.dalemayer.com

Twitter – @DaleMayer

Facebook Page – geni.us/DaleMayerFBFanPage

Facebook Group – geni.us/DaleMayerFBGroup

BookBub – geni.us/DaleMayerBookbub

Instagram – geni.us/DaleMayerInstagram

Goodreads – geni.us/DaleMayerGoodreads

Newsletter – geni.us/DaleNews

Printed in the USA
CPSIA information can be obtained
at www.ICGtesting.com
CBHW052023081124
17086CB00006BA/83

9 781778 864803